CAMERON 7

JADE JONES

WEBSITE

www.jadedpublications.com

JOIN OUR NEWSLETTER

Text *BOOKS* to 44144

CAMERON 8 IS OUT NOW!

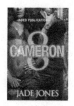

PROLOGUE

Jude barely made it to ground transportation before his cellphone started blowing up. He had just powered it on after being in airplane mode. This time the caller was not Michael. In fact, it was his protégée, Magyc.

As soon as Jude answered, Magyc started talking a mile a minute. The young cat was so frantic that Jude could barely make out a word he was saying. "Hol' up, slow down. What happened?"

"I need you to get to Emory Hospital." Magyc's voice cracked as he spoke. He was so upset that he wanted to murder someone—anyone.

"Aight. I'm on my way, man." Jude hung up the phone and put a little more pep in his step. He knew something was wrong by the sound of Magyc's voice. This night couldn't get any worse.

"Is everything okay?" Cameron asked in concern.

"Yes, everything's fine," Jude lied. "Just got a lil' business to handle and then I promise I'll come back to you."

Cameron didn't like the sound of that. For some reason, hearing him say it made her feel like she would never see him again. Jude was telling her everything was okay, but she had a feeling it wasn't.

When Cam and Jude finally made it back to his home, he made

sure she was comfortable, left her with a loaded 9mm, kissed her on the forehead, and told her he loved her more than himself.

"I love you too, Jude. Please be careful...and please try to hurry back."

"I'll do my best," he assured her.

Jude left the house around 4:30 in the morning and headed downtown to *Emory*. He found Magyc, Michael, and a few of their men in a hospital room. Jude was shocked to see Roxie hooked up to a breathing machine. A heart monitor positioned beside the bed was the only proof she was still living. She looked bad—really bad. Now Jag had gone too fucking far.

"I'ma kill the mothafucka," Magyc said with tears in his eyes. "I'ma kill him."

Jude stood in the doorway in silence. Jag was supposed to be his. But seeing Roxie lying there helpless made him feel like Magyc deserved to off him.

"She lost the baby..." Magyc's voice trembled with anger. "A nigga ain't even know she was pregnant. She didn't tell me..." He shook his head. "And now I gotta explain to Briana's family why their daughter's dead. This shit's all bad. It's fucked up, bruh. I should've been there. I should've fuckin' been there. If she doesn't make it, I—"

"Don't put that shit out there in the universe," Jude said. "She's gonna pull through. Roxie's strong and you know it."

Guilt consumed Magyc. He hated that he hadn't given a hundred percent of himself to her. He hated that he'd ever lied to and hurt her. Roxie was his baby, his everything. He couldn't lose her. Not like this.

Magyc promised himself that when she finally woke up from her coma, he would marry her. He didn't care that he was only twenty-two. He wanted to spend his life with her. But first and foremost, he had to put Jag in a casket.

"I'ma get at that nigga," Magyc said. "On life. I'ma end that nigga's existence."

JUDE LEFT the hospital around 5 in the morning. With everything going on, he wanted to get back to Cameron as fast as he could. He ran a couple red lights in order to make it home in haste.

Jude was surprised when he noticed the gates to his house opened. Sadly, he had never fixed the system. "Shit!" Jude punched the steering wheel after remembering that Jag knew about the glitch. All he had to do was push 0 to mosey inside. "This is not happening!"

Jude parked his car crookedly before hopping out. His heart thumped wildly inside his chest. He knew shit was real the minute he saw his front door cracked open.

Jude snatched his gun out and ran through the home. As expected, Cameron and the children were nowhere to be found. They were gone. Just like that. Jude wasn't even away a full two hours and they were gone. His heart broke when he saw the 9mm on the hallway floor. A few furniture pieces were overturned, which indicated a struggle.

"FUCK!" Jude punched a hole in the nearby wall. His knuckles tore open and bled but he didn't notice or care. The only thing on his mind was the fact that Jag had gained the upper hand. *How the hell I let this motherfucker catch me slipping*, he asked himself.

All of a sudden, Jude's cellphone rang. He recognized the number immediately. "Bitch nigga, I made you! I could break you too," Jude threatened.

Jag laughed, clearly amused. "I won."

Jude finally calmed down after remembering he had his wife and son. "Jag? Jag, listen to me. Our beef ain't got shit to do with Cameron. Leave her out of this, man."

"What the fuck are you talking about? It's got everything to do with Cameron," Jag reminded him. "My mother...Lark...my little sister. You don't recall that? It was all for Cam, am I right?"

"Jag, look, I never hurt Alessia. That's on everything I love. She got away, dawg. She's still out there."

"You're lying," Jag denied. Due to his mental disassociation, he didn't know what was real and what was fake. His sister could've been alive, but he had a feeling Jude was bullshitting.

"I'm not lying! She's alive!"

"I may be a killer, but at least I take responsibility for the fucked up things I've done," Jag said. "You took my family away from me... now I'm taking yours..."

Click.

Jag disconnected the call, and Jude launched his phone in anger. "Dammit!" His hands trembled uncontrollably. He didn't know what to do.

Suddenly, Jude remembered the test results on his office's desk. A part of him still wasn't ready to learn the truth, but at the very least he deserved to know.

Jude walked inside the spacious room and stopped in front of his desk. Now that the answer was at his fingertips, he was anxious to find out. With shaky hands, he grabbed the envelope, tore it open, and read the letter.

Journee was 99.6% Jude's daughter. Tears fell from his eyes as he read the results over and over.

That mothafucka has to be stopped, he convinced himself. One way or another, Jag was going in the ground.

Jude cocked his gun, tucked it in his waistline, and left the room on a mission....

1

___

Two Months Later

C ameron gently trailed her French tips along Jude's soft skin. Her body felt so warm against his as she snuggled against him. When she wrapped her arm around his midsection, he pulled her closer.

Moonlight poured into their bedroom as they slept in a gold Italian king size bed. The sweet, fruity scent of her lotion filled his nose. Her smell and touch was intoxicating.

"I love you, Cam," he murmured.

She stirred a little but didn't speak.

"You hear me?" he asked.

Silence.

"Cam?"

Suddenly, Jude woke up in a cold sweat and realized her side of the bed was empty. He ran a hand over the cool spot on his mattress where his wife usually occupied. He missed her presence. He missed her laughter. He missed the smell of her hair, the way her body melted into his whenever they spooned.

Two months felt like two whole eternities. He and his niggas had been combing the streets looking for Cam, but they always came up empty-handed.

Jude contemplated falling back to sleep. Maybe he'd luck up and see her again his dreams. As tempting as it was, he knew he wouldn't drift off into slumber again. It already wasn't often that he slept. It was hard to when you weren't with the one you loved.

The entire house was quiet—eerily quiet. No evidence that he even had a family. Jude would've given anything just to hear his infant cry. What he put himself through everyday...that shit wasn't life. It wasn't living... He merely existed.

Jude thought about copping an ounce or two of coke to help him relax, but decided against it. He'd kicked his nasty drug habit over a year ago and wasn't keen on relapsing.

All of a sudden, he heard the sound of movement from the front of his house. Automatically, he grabbed the twin thumpers resting on his nightstand and climbed out the bed. He didn't close his eyes without them nearby. Paranoia had completely taken hold of his life ever since the kidnappings.

Jude cautiously made his way towards the noise, making sure to keep his own undetected. The sounds grew louder as he neared the front of the house. Someone was definitely in his crib.

All of the lights were off, and the home was blanketed in total darkness. Yet, if he popped he still wouldn't miss. A killer had those instincts. Jude's grip on his suppressed pistol tightened. Had Jag returned to finish the job he started?

The minute Jude saw a dark figure lurking in the family room he raised his gun and took aim.

"Wait, bruh, don't shoot! It's me!" Magyc said in slurred speech. He was Jude's 22-year old protégée and good friend. A menace to society, most of his youth had been spent in juvie. However, he was exceptionally book smart. Jude saw a little of himself in Magyc, like the little brother he never had.

Magyc was lifted off Henny and Percocet. He hadn't been sober once since the day Roxie was rushed to the emergency room. She was still in a coma and her health was really beginning to take a toll on him. Not only that, but he felt tremendous guilt for what happened to Briana.

Magyc made the mistake of attending his ex's funeral, and it took six men to pull her father and brother off him. Magyc's life was spiraling out of control after Jag's heartless actions. The only thing that could offer the young misfit peace was putting a bullet in that mothafucka's head.

Magyc stumbled a little before collapsing next to the couch. At 22, he was 5"10 and slender, yet toned in frame. His skin was cognac-colored and his dreads reached a little past his shoulders. There was a thuggish charm about him.

Magyc was too zooted to stand up on his own. He couldn't even drive his car after leaving the strip club. One of the dancers he fucked with occasionally had to drop him off.

Jude quickly rushed to his aid. He'd almost forgotten that his Protégé owned a spare key to his private estate. If it weren't for Magyc speaking up when he did, Jude would've blindly put a bullet in his head without a second thought. Both men were losing themselves.

Jude carefully helped his intoxicated friend onto the ivory button tufted sofa. It was a $2000 piece of furniture, but he didn't bother removing Magyc's Jordans. By the time the 22-year old's face hit the cushion he was snoring.

Now that his nerves were put at ease, Jude went to the kitchen and poured himself a shot of Remy. One turned into two, and two soon turned into four.

Jude released a deep sigh and ran his hands through his dreads. "Damn, Cameron... Where the fuck you at, baby? Give a nigga a sign... Shit..."

After five back-to-back shots, he staggered out the kitchen and into the family room. Magyc was dead to the world, as he lay stretched out across the sofa.

Jude sank into the chair across from him, and rested the guns in his lap. He made sure to keep his finger on the trigger. Reclining his head, Jude slowly closed his eyes. Images of Cameron's beautiful face flood his mind as he drifted off to sleep.

All of a sudden, his phone started ringing, causing him to jerk awake. Jude quickly answered it, surprised that the caller was Magyc's brother and his accountant, Michael.

"Hey, wassup, man? Everything cool?" Jude asked, with concern heavy in his tone.

It was four in the morning. The last time Michael called at that hour it was to let him know that their precious warehouse had been torched.

"I'm on my way to you right now," Michael said. "I just got a tip on where Cam and the kids might be."

2

Two and a half hours later, Jude, Magyc, and Michael pulled into the lot of a murky *Econo Lodge Inn* out in Columbus, Georgia. Several cars were scattered on the premises, but none of them looked like one Jag would drive. Was he being low key for the sake of staying under the radar?

"How you come up on this tip?" Jude asked Michael. He wanted to have hope that Cameron was inside, but it seemed very unlikely. Jag was smart—smarter than the average. Smarter than Jude ever gave him credit for. Why the hell would he hole up in some crummy, sub-par motel two hours outside the city?

"My patnah owns it. He hit me up sayin' a chick matchin' her description showed up with some white boy."

"And you think it's her?"

There was a glimmer of doubt in Michael's eyes. He looked like an older version of Magyc but without the dreads and mural of tattoos. "...He described her to a tee, man," he said, rather uncertainly.

Jude accepted his answer for what it was.

Michael parked the Mercedes truck and together they all climbed out.

Out of nowhere, Magyc keeled over and vomited. On the entire ride over he was silent and now Jude understood why. The 22-year old was still twisted from last night.

Magyc had a terrible hangover and should've stayed his ass home, but he insisted on helping. The business was slowly crumbling at the hands of Jag, and someone had to have Jude's back when shit got real. However, he was pretty much useless now.

Jude looked at his protégée in a disapproving way. "Aye, bruh, you good?" He felt a prickle of annoyance that Magyc wasn't in tip-top shape. He needed him now more than ever—more so for support than protection. They didn't involve the police in Cam's disappearance because they wanted to handle Jag on their own, accordingly.

Magyc wiped his mouth with the back of his hand. There were tiny specks of throw up on his distressed Yeezy sweatshirt. He looked like shit but he was unable to be talked down.

"I'm good," he said weakly.

Jude looked at Magyc doubtfully, yet held his tongue. He then diverted his attention to the second-rate motel that may or may not be sheltering his family. The trio stepped inside and walked rather tentatively to the front desk.

Michael didn't even have to utter a single word to the concierge. It was like they had a silent understanding, because the key to Cameron's room was automatically slid across the counter. Jude collected it and together they braved the hotel, in search of his wife.

Once they reached room 308, Jude's heart sank and a dry lump formed in his throat. Beyond the door could've been anything—maybe even something he wasn't ready to see.

What if Jag had hurt his children? Dozens of unpleasant thoughts ran through his mind as he stood frozen. He didn't know what to expect. He didn't know what to look forward to. The only thing Jude anticipated was putting a bullet in Jag's head. That mothafucka had a hollow point with his name written all over it for the grief he'd caused.

God, I don't come clambering to you often, but please let my family be safe and sound, he prayed. *I'll do anything. Just grant me this one favor, this one time.*

Jude took a deep, shuddering breath before placing his hand over the knob. Michael and Magyc both had their chromes in their grip, ready to pop if need be. He was just about to stick the key card in when Magyc's knees buckled and he fell against the frame. He didn't collapse fully, but it was clear he was in poor condition. He was losing himself and his self-control on life.

"Why don't you go back to the car," Jude suggested. His tone was ripe with suppressed irritation.

"Nah, I'm good. I'm good," Magyc said, straightening up. He tried to shake off the effects of his hangover. That'd be the last time he mixed drugs and liquor.

Both men looked weary of his ability to handle a gun while in such weak state.

Jude shrugged off the distraction anyway and swiped the key card. The door beeped green, granting him access. His heart hung on the edge of suspense. Swallowing his anxiety, Jude pushed the door open slowly and walked in first—

He quickly shielded his eyes and looked away from the disgustingly repulsive sight before him.

3

"Aaaaaaahhhhh!"

A high-pitched scream rang out after all three men barged in on a Coprophiliac being pleasured on the floor. Beneath his naked body was a plastic sheet to catch the waste spilling from his paid prostitute.

"Who the fuck are ya'll! GET THE FUCK OUT!" she hollered.

As soon as the trick saw them he quickly jumped up and covered his dick in shame. He didn't know if he was more embarrassed that they walked in or that he was married. At first he thought his wife might've even sent them.

"What the fuck...?"

The space reeked of sweat and shit. A real fucking stench trench. Magyc and Michael gaped silently at the offensive image in front of them. Magyc clutched his stomach, and fought the urge to vomit again. Michael pinched his nostrils closed so that he wouldn't have to smell it. What they saw was revolting and flat out sickening.

The bitch certainly wasn't Cameron—even though she *did* have a keen likeness to her. They shared the same complexion and body type, but there was no resemblance when it came to class and etiquette. Cam wouldn't have been caught dead doing some foul shit like that.

"Who the hell are they, John! I told you I don't do group rates!" she yelled.

John's cheeks turned a rosy pink. He faltered in response. "I—I—"

WHAM!

Jude cracked his trifling ass with the gun, busting his shit wide open. John fell backwards onto the cheap bed and grabbed his bloody lips. Someone had to suffer for the misunderstanding, and he just so happened to be standing the closest.

Forlorn shrieking pierced the air after the prostitute saw the guns. Three hundred dollars certainly wasn't worth losing her life. She never signed up for this shit.

Magyc and Michael looked at Jude like he had lost it. They weren't accustomed to his blustery temper. Not a single person in the room expected him to fly off the handle like that.

"SHUT THE FUCK UP! Shut yo' mothafuckin' cocksucker right now 'fore I put somethin' in it!" Spit flew everywhere as Jude pointed the rawlo at her head. His index finger rested on the trigger. He was two seconds away from squeezing and rocking her ass to sleep just because.

The frightened woman quickly slammed her mouth shut, fearful for her life. It was obvious that Jude was a loose cannon. He was beyond pissed that his wife and children weren't there. He was even more upset that he walked in on some shit he didn't need to see. What a waste of fucking energy and effort.

"Damn, my fault, 'cuz," Michael said with quiet conviction. He could see the hurt, agitation, and disappointment all over Jude's face. He felt for him—especially since his family had fallen victim to the same ill fate. "I thought she was here. He described Cam to a tee. My bad though, man. You can put this all on me."

In a blind rage, Jude rushed Michael, slammed him against the wall, and pressed his gun to his temple. "You gotdamn right I'mma put this shit on you! Nigga, I should blow yo' mothafuckin' head off for wastin' my gotdamn time!" The veins around his temples were alarmingly swollen. Jude was heated that they didn't find his family.

"Aye, chill the fuck out!" Magyc said, coming to his brother's defense. "Ain't nobody finna fuckin' shoot nobody! It ain't his mothafuckin' fault! He lost his family too!" he reminded Jude. "Don't you see we givin' that fuck nigga exactly what he wants! To have us panickin' and turnin' on each other and shit."

The silence in the room swelled ominously.

Jude slowly lowered his gun. Magyc was right.

On the entire ride over he had serious doubts that Cameron was there, but once they arrived at the motel he felt a tiny shred of hope. Now he was crushed with disappointment. It felt like he'd walked in his home and saw that Cam and the kids were gone all over again. The pain and loneliness was overwhelming. It was slowly eating away at his sanity like an infectious disease. Life felt like it was playing its cruelest joke on him.

Jude turned to the man lying on the bed with a busted mouth. He could no longer suppress his curiosity. "What the fuck turns you on about that nasty ass shit?"

The john cringed in fear. He was too scared to even speak.

"Never mind. Don't even answer that shit."

With nothing left to say, Jude walked restlessly out the room and back to the parking lot. The moment he felt the cool breeze hit his skin, he dropped to his knees right there on the ground. He felt like the weight of the world was on his shoulders.

For the first time ever, he imagined how much peace it would bring if he just put the gun to his head and pulled the trigger. Then again, that'd be giving Jag exactly what he wanted.

Jude looked up at the pale blue sky with weary eyes. Stress was etched in his expression. He hadn't been the same since Cam and the children left.

Will I ever see my family again, he wondered.

As of now, the chances seemed highly unlikely. And Jude was slowly losing faith in himself and those around him. Something had to give.

WITH A LOOK OF COOL DISTASTE, Cameron watched Jag screw a suppressor onto a Glock 17. He then covered the weapon in bubble wrap and placed it in a cardboard box to ship to himself. He was on his way to complete an assignment—the first since he'd dragged her to a secluded log cabin out in Mineral Bluff, Georgia.

Cam figured he must've been running low on funds. That was the only time he ever fulfilled contracts. Otherwise, he sat at home, forcing her to play out his sick, twisted fantasy of being a family.

Jag had purchased the cabin fully furnished and move-in ready. It was tucked off in the woods, away from general population, and anyone that could possibly hear her screaming. It was a nice home that featured 3 bedrooms, a hot tub, pool table, arcade, fire pit, and deck that overlooked the beautiful sunsets. However, it felt like sheer hell to Cameron.

She was living her worst nightmare, literally. Two whole months of being his slave and sex toy was torture. Every day she opened her eyes her hatred for Jag increased more and more. She couldn't wait for the day she got her hands on one of his guns.

Cameron stared meditatively at him. "Who's going to take care of my babies when you're gone?" she asked, miserably. Cam wouldn't dare refer to them as his children. Jag wasn't a father figure or a man at all. He was a fucking monster—a savage, untamed beast.

This was the first time Cameron had spoken to him in weeks. Normally, she just ignored whatever he said and pretended he didn't exist—even during sex. The normal person would've eventually gotten bored with her, but not Jag. He wasn't affected by Cam's aloofness or snobbish attitude. His crazy ass had deluded himself into believing it was only temporary, and that eventually she'd fall in love with him again.

Jag was out of his mothafucking mind, but that had been decided a while ago.

"Do you hear me?" she said, once he didn't answer. Cam stared inquiringly at him as she waited on a response.

He seemed deeply interested in what guns he would bring with him on his trip. Like those who walked the path of his career before him, Jag took great pleasure in his work. Only someone who didn't have a soul or conscience could do what he did.

Cam would've given anything to grab the gun he was holding, put it in his mouth, and pull the trigger.

That was how much she hated his ass.

Jag was a professional hit-for-hire—the self-proclaimed best. Unfortunately, Cameron didn't find out until it was too late. For months he lied to her, claiming he made his living from a restaurant he and his mom co-owned. However, when his true colors started surfacing the truth came out about him being a contract killer.

Cameron felt like she didn't even know Jag. She damn sure didn't recognize him now. It was inhumane to hold her and her children captive. It was barbaric.

"I hear you...I just don't feel inclined to answer you," he said, smugly. Jag didn't look up as he continued packing shit in his suitcase.

Cam caught him toss a box of condoms inside and became disgusted. Everything about his ass was so fucking repulsive. "I need to be un-cuffed if you're leaving!" she demanded.

Jag kept her secured to the bed damn near 24 hours a day. He didn't even allow her to take care of her own kids. The only time he ever freed her was to have his way, let her use the bathroom, or to grant her time to stretch and get her blood circulating. He didn't want her getting deep vein thrombosis and dying on him.

"You don't need to do shit but pray I come back in a good mood," he threatened.

After slamming his suitcase shut, Jag walked out of the bedroom.

"What if I have to use the bathroom?" Cam called out after him.

Jag stopped suddenly in his tracks. His heartless response made her despise him even more.

"I'll worry about the mess when I get back," he said, firmly.

"Jag, please!" she begged. "At least let me use the bathroom before you go. I don't even know how long you'll be gone."

He breathed a sigh of frustration and carefully thought about it. To her satisfaction, he nodded. "I guess..."

Slugging over to the bed, he pulled the keys out and un-cuffed her. The first thing Cameron did was rub her sore arms. "C'mon. Let's go. I have a flight to catch," he said, rather annoyed.

Cameron slowly climbed out the bed. From the corner of her eye, she peeped the pen lying on the wooden night table.

Jag gave her back a light push as if telling her to walk faster. He knew she was stalling, because she hated being bound to the bed. But until she stopped trying to run, that was how things had to be.

Cameron stepped inside the adjoined bathroom. She started to close the door behind her but Jag quickly stopped her with his hand. "Damn, can I get some fucking privacy?! You don't have to hover over me every time I take a piss! This is fucking ridiculous!" she lashed out.

Jag looked at her sharply. "Use the toilet or use the bed. Doesn't matter to me," he said, nonchalantly.

Cameron sucked her teeth and sauntered to the toilet. Jag fired up a cigarette while he waited. He saw the unspoken criticism in her eyes. He knew how she felt about him without her even having to say it.

Cam scanned her surroundings. There were three separate windows but they were all sealed shut with caulk.

"Stop looking for a way out, Cam. There is none." He'd read her mind and knew exactly what she was planning.

Cameron wanted to cry. "People are probably out there looking for me, Jag. How long are you gonna do this shit? You can't keep me locked up in here forever. This is crazy!"

His face was unexpressive. She couldn't tell what was going through his demented head.

"For however long I feel its necessary."

She met his eyes calmly. "Jag, please—"

"I have to go soon, Cam," he replied, brusquely. "Finish up. I don't have all fucking day."

After wiping herself, she flushed the toilet, and washed her hands. She felt like she was walking back to her dreaded prison cell as she approached the bed. Jag was nice enough to leave the TV on most days, yet she hardly paid any attention to it.

Jag pulled out the keys to the cuffs—

Suddenly, Cam grabbed the pen off the night table and jammed it in his shoulder.

"*Aaah, shit*! You bitch!"

WHAP!

Jag slapped her so hard that she fell and hit her head on the edge of the bed frame. The blow temporarily left her dazed and confused for a second. Blood leaked from her nose and ran into her mouth.

From her peripheral, she noticed a paperclip lying underneath the bed.

Jag yanked her towards him by her leg, but not before she grabbed it. With his free hand, he snatched the pen out, and yelped in pain. Cam thought he might actually stab her, but was surprised when he tossed it instead.

"Why do you keep doing this shit?!" he yelled. "I don't wanna fucking hurt you! All I wanna do is love you! That's all I ever wanted to do was love you, Cam!" His eyes softened and his face was almost earnest enough to convince her. "Why the fuck don't you wanna love me?"

Cameron looked in the depths of his stormy blue eyes. "It's a thin ass line between love and hate."

She could tell that wasn't the answer Jag was hoping for. His dignity was offended. Much to his intense irritation, she just wouldn't comply. Grabbing Cam by the neck, he snatched her up and threw her onto the bed. She tried to kick him, but he quickly climbed on top and held her down.

"Jag, STOP! Enough is enough! I cannot take this shit! This ain't no fucking way to live! Please let me go! I swear I will never tell a soul! I put that on my parents! Please, Jag. All I wanna do is take care of my babies!" she cried.

Ignoring her pleas, he handcuffed her to the bed so that she couldn't escape. Once she was secured, he grabbed her face and kissed her. Cam bit his tongue so hard that she drew blood.

"Ah!"

Jag pulled his hand back to slap her but stopped mid-strike. Regardless of how much she fought him, he really was trying to love her. He didn't want to beat on her anymore. He had gotten tired of doing that shit. All he wanted was for her to love him again.

Jag wiped the blood off his bottom lip and climbed off her. "I'll let that one slide," he said.

She spit in his direction but missed. "I hate yo' mothafucking ass!" Disheveled hair and smeared blood on her face made Cam look crazy.

He chuckled, amused by her antics. He felt all of her anguish, but was not dismayed by it.

Cameron watched as he grabbed his suitcase and headed to the door. "Jag, no, wait! Who's gonna look after the kids?" she cried. "They can't take care of themselves!"

Silence was the response she received. He didn't feel obligated to explain a damn thing to her. "Jag, I'm sorry! Please! I'm so sorry about everything! Don't take it out on the kids! Please just let me go!"

"Goodbye, Cameron."

"What about my babies, Jag?! You're just gonna leave and not answer me? Don't just fucking walk away from me! You hear me, dammit! ANSWER ME! JAG!"

Cameron's screams went ignored after he slammed and locked the door behind him. Forty-eight hours alone in solitude without knowing the state of her children's well-being was enough to make her go insane.

Enraged, Cameron continued to shout and curse at Jag until her voice went hoarse. "You're a mothafucking coward! You hear me?! I hope yo' ass get fucked up over there! Stupid, loony ass mothafucka! You deserve the same pain you inflict! I pray yo' ass die, bitch! *That's* what I pray for every mothafucking night!"

Outside the bedroom, Rebecca stared incredulously at the closed door. She was the 32-year old nanny Jag hired to look after the children while he was away. She was a light-skinned woman with bushy, nut-brown hair, and thick-framed glasses.

Since Cameron was locked up in the bedroom she didn't know that Jag already had someone on the job. He couldn't trust Cam to do anything, because every opportunity she got she used to attack him or try to escape. Jag had to keep her ass locked away 24/7 like she was in a maximum-security prison.

Jag pretended he didn't hear Cameron screaming and yelling all sorts of obscenities. Eventually, she would tire herself out. Rebecca, on the other hand, seemed disturbed by it.

"Is everything okay?" she asked in a non-confrontational tone. She didn't want to seem nosey, but she'd have to be deaf not to hear the chaos inside the bedroom. It was clear they had some serious familial issues.

Jag waved it off. "Everything's fine," he said. "Now look, you're welcome to anything you see. Feel free to make yourself at home. *Mi casa su casa*. All I ask is that you do me one, small favor... Don't touch that door. Don't go near it. Hell, don't even look at it. You think you can do that for me?"

Apprehension swept her features. Rebecca saw pure madness when she looked in Jag's eyes. She had a growing sense of unease just being there. She was afraid of him. If it weren't for the fact that he was paying her handsomely she wouldn't have been dealing with his crazy ass. Still, she had an intense desire to know what the hell was going on.

"Why? Who's in there? Is that the mother—"

"How 'bout I toss in an extra grand if you don't ask me any questions." Her inquisitiveness would only lead to her demise if she didn't mind her fucking business.

"Agreed," she said quickly.

Jag was already paying her $2,000 just to babysit for two days. The cabin could've caught on fire and she still wouldn't have touched that door to help. Rebecca needed the money, and was willing to look the other way this one time to get it.

Before Jag left he kissed his daughter, Journee goodbye. She was starting to look more and more like Cameron by the day. Justin, on the other hand, got no love since he wasn't biologically his son. Jag would've flipped if he found out Journee wasn't either. Luckily, Jude was the only one who knew the truth.

"I'll see you soon." Jag headed to the front door and then stopped suddenly. "And don't forget what I told you, Becky," he said. "Remember...curiosity killed the cat..."

4

Juicy grunted and stirred awake after hearing Wayne's phone vibrate on the nightstand. She knew it was his nagging ass wife without even having to look at the phone screen.

An uneasy chill sat on her heart. Every time Tabitha called, Juicy was reminded that Wayne wasn't fully hers. She loved him more than anything—possibly more than herself, but the messy shit they were doing would only lead to heartbreak, and she knew it.

Recently, Juicy found out that he had a whole wife and family at home. For several months, Wayne bullshitted about being single. He never wore his ring, and he even told her that he didn't have children.

Juicy naively listened to every single lie that tumbled from his sexy, thick lips. To make matters worse, she fell in love with his cheating ass. She had met him while dancing at *Secret's Gentlemen's Club* on the west side of Cleveland.

Normally, she didn't commingle with customers, but something about Wayne was different. He had more appeal than any man she'd ever met. Something about him drew her in like a moth to a flame. He was professional, polished, chivalrous, and a different type from the thugs she normally dated.

Wayne was a well-respected brain surgeon who worked down at

Cleveland Clinic, and his wife a pediatrician. His family and friends would've shunned him if they knew he was fooling around with a stripper. Only it was more than just an affair—at least, for Juicy it was. Her feelings were strongly invested after six months of fooling around. And as silly as it sounded, she had hope that he'd one day leave his wife of 15 years.

Wayne told her regularly that they were getting a divorce soon, but soon never came. He failed to mention the prenuptial that was never signed, so the chances that he really would were slim.

"Your phone," Juicy said, nudging him.

Wayne grunted but didn't wake.

"Wayne, get your fucking phone! That bitch is calling! You really don't hear that shit though, my nigga?" she yelled. Her tone was laced with irritation.

He immediately jerked up and grabbed his iPhone. "Damn. Why'd you let me sleep late?" he complained.

"Nigga, I'm not your fucking alarm!" she hissed.

Wayne slapped her naked booty cheek as a penalty for being sassy. She knew how he felt about that ghetto, smart-mouthed shit, but she still tried him. Juicy was totally unfazed. She'd been stripping for years. She was used to niggas smacking her ass hard on the regular.

Wayne ran a hand over his gray and silver hair as he stared blankly at his phone screen. The texture of it was soft and silky like he had Spanish in his bloodline.

Wayne was an attractive man, beautiful even. His smooth skin was the color of bronze. He had soft gray eyes, a dimpled chin, and a perfectly chiseled face. Juicy often told him he looked like Rick Fox.

"I'm 'bout to answer. Keep quiet for a sec," he said.

Juicy looked at his ass like he was nuts. *Did this mothafucka really just tell me to keep quiet? Like I'd deliberately talk knowing that cuntbag is on the phone. I don't know how much more of this shit I can take.*

Wayne stood from the bed naked and went to the bathroom. He was 45-years old, looked 30, and had the athletic build and stamina of a man in his early 20s. It was no secret that Wayne had turned her young ass out.

He made her bust on the regular, bought her expensive clothes and shoes, and treated her to fancy trips overseas. Aside from the sex and materialistic shit, he added value to her life by teaching her things and instilling a wisdom that was far beyond her years. Unfortunately, she didn't have the sense to leave him alone. Juicy had become so smitten and dependent on Wayne that she completely forgot what they were doing was wrong. A woman's nightly companion shouldn't have been someone else's husband. Juicy told herself that repeatedly. Yet any time she made an effort to leave him, something caused her to stay.

All she heard was, "Calm down, lemme talk," before the bathroom door closed shut.

Juicy rolled over and looked up at the tray ceiling in her bedroom. Wayne rented her a spacious condo on W. Lakeside Avenue, and got her a cute little BMW to push around the city, but both were in his name. Wayne treated her good; yet, at the end of the day she was his property. If she left, she couldn't take any of it with her. It was the unspoken agreement they shared.

After several minutes, he finally reemerged from the bathroom with a look of satisfaction on his face. That must've meant he found an acceptable lie to feed his significant other. He nourished his wife and side chick's insecurities with the same game and finesse, and they bought it every single time.

Juicy seemed unmoved when he climbed back in the bed next to her. He tried to kiss her, but she hastily turned away.

"Don't come in here trying to pacify me, Wayne."

"What the fuck do you want me to do? Ignore her so she can keep calling? I had to tell her something—"

"We wouldn't even be in this situation if you just got the damn divorce—"

"I told you, I'm working on it. Divorces are expensive."

"Nigga, so is this condo. And them trips out the country we take. And the Rolls Royce you just got that bitch for her birthday."

Juicy only knew what car it was because she stalked his wife's Instagram regularly just to hate. She wanted to know how Wayne had her living—which was far more extravagant and fancier than what he did for her. Juicy couldn't help but be jealous. Tabitha was his wife, but she felt like she could give him so much more.

Wayne told Juicy everything that was wrong in his marriage. He confided and vented to her like a patient to a counselor. His wife didn't listen, she never had the energy or time to fuck, and she was no longer as passionate as she was when they first married. He claimed they only stayed together for the sake of the children. He also didn't want to disappoint or offend her father who'd helped get him the high-paying position he now had. To put it simply, he was obligated to Tabitha, whether he wanted to admit it or not.

"You shouldn't even be worrying yourself about her possessions. That materialistic shit doesn't mean anything. You should be focused on us. What we have is far greater in value than some damn car."

She broke in anxiously. "But—"

"Look at me," Wayne insisted.

Juicy kept her focus on the floor-to-ceiling windows in her bedroom. She could see Lake Erie from her condo. He had her spoiled, but she wanted more. She wanted the ring, the title, and him all wrapped in one.

"You're so damn pretty when you mad. You know that?" He kissed her neck. "Huh?" He kissed her shoulder.

Juicy didn't respond, and he just admired her in silence. She was coffee-brown with chinky hazel eyes, sooty lashes, and deep dimples. The left half of her hair was shaved with two small lines cut into the side. She sported a gold hoop in her nose, and three stars were tattooed on the side of her temple. She was a beautiful girl, but hood at heart. That's what initially attracted him to her. Juicy was the complete opposite of his upstanding wife.

When Juicy didn't turn her head, Wayne gently grabbed her chin, and forced her to look in his eyes. He was devilishly handsome.

Damn, why can't I leave this nigga alone, she asked herself. *He ain't even mine.*

Juicy had let things go too far. She was in too deep, and there was no turning back now.

Wayne's gray eyes stared worshipfully at her. "You know I wanna be with you, Diana. But you gotta be patient. I'm trying. Just work with me." He was the only man in her life that called her by her real name. He didn't like using her stripper pseudonym. As a matter of fact, he'd made her hang her heels up permanently. Since he took care of her financial needs, Juicy agreed. Wayne came into her life and completely changed her ways and habits.

"I'm tired of being patient." There was a bitter loneliness twining around her heart. She wanted to sleep next to him every night without disturbance.

Wayne kissed her heart-shaped lips. "I promise it'll all be worth it in the end."

"Whatever, mothafucka. You have no intentions of really leaving that bitch and you know it."

"Why would I wanna spend my life with someone that makes me unhappy? I don't love her anymore. I'm in love with you. Stop telling yourself that I'll never leave her."

"You won't."

Wayne bit her bottom lip and tugged it with his teeth. He hated whenever she went against what he said. "Don't argue with me," he told her. "Besides, I gotta get ready for work soon." He weaseled between her thighs, his wood was already hard and leaking with pre cum. "Let me get you off before I go."

Juicy tried to hide the smile that broke free. He was so giving, financially and sexually.

"I don't want none," she said, knowing damn well she did.

Wayne pinned her arms high above her head and pressed the tip of his bare dick against her base. Juicy squirmed and moaned. He had a donkey dick, every time felt like the first time.

"Let me in," he whispered in her hair.

Juicy tried to relax as she allowed him to bury all 10-inches inside. After filling her up with his porno dick, Wayne started hitting it in a slow, circular rhythm. He wrapped a massive hand around her slender neck to hold her in place. He didn't want her running from the dick like she always did.

"Wayne, oh my God!" Her voice was a thrilling whisper. "Get it, daddy! Shit! Make me cum!"

He snaked his tongue in her mouth and kissed like they had made vows. "You love me?" he asked. "Say you love me, baby."

"I love you, daddy!" she cried out. Her moans were loud enough to wake the dead.

Wayne pulled out, climbed down at her waist, and buried his face deep in her pussy. He licked, sucked, chewed, and nibbled on her button until her legs trembled and she came. He knew his head game was crazy. It was her weakness.

After making her nut, Wayne crawled out the bed and proceeded to dress. He told her he had to get ready for work, but she knew he really just had to get his ass back home to Tabitha.

Wayne kissed Juicy goodbye, tossed her a little spending money, and departed. Once again, she was left alone in bed with a wet pussy and empty heart.

5

That night Jude woke up in a cold sweat again from nightmares of Cam and the kids being taken. His dreams were even more vivid than the real thing. In his nightmares, there was blood all over the walls and heinous laughter in the background. It was like a bad acid trip.

Jag would've been pleased with himself to know he was the man responsible for why Jude couldn't sleep peacefully. Aside from costing him millions of dollars after setting his warehouse on fire, Jag had caused irreparable emotional damage. People were dead and his family was still out there somewhere.

Jude looked around his dark bedroom and suddenly broke down. It'd been years since he cried. He didn't even shed a tear at his own mother's funeral. He felt so broken and deserted without Cam. He had an army of loyal soldiers on his team, but he had never felt more alone until now. He was suffering from severe depression. Life just wasn't worth living without his baby.

After a brief period of lamenting, Jude wiped his tears, and grabbed his gun and car keys. His house was completely empty that evening. Normally, Magyc slept over every night, but he was obviously still in his feelings about Jude putting a gun to his brother's head.

Jude's entire empire was slowly collapsing before his very eyes. He was losing control and it was all because of that piece of a man Cameron just couldn't stay away from.

I should've never let that pussy nigga breathe, he said to himself. *I should've buried that mothafucka with his brother a long ass time ago. Back when I first found out he was fucking with Cam. Why did I ever spare that bitch?*

Jude hopped in his 'Rari, blasted the newest Jay Rock album, and skirted off. It was only 1 am, but he couldn't sleep. He needed to clear his head, and maybe even have a drink or two.

After aimlessly driving around twenty minutes, he ended up outside the bar Essence worked at. Kendrick's voice poured through the custom speakers as he passionately rapped the chorus.

Big money, big booty bitches...
Man, that shit gon' be the death of me...
Big problems, I must admit it...
Man, that shit gon' be the death of me...

USING HIS TRUSTY CROWBAR, Jag focused on breaking inside his target's home through the front door. Ralph Tompkins Jr. lived in a cozy ranch style house out in Reno, Nevada. He had no idea that his time on Earth had run out.

After prying the door open, Jag gave it a gentle push with a gloved hand. His suppressed pistol entered the house before he did. He looked like the boogey man in a black duster coat, black skullcap, and black utility boots. It was the simple wardrobe of a man who wanted to blend in with the night. His face was unwelcoming. He was all about business that night.

Jag heard classical music playing in the den. He decided to investigate. The faster he finished the job the sooner he could get back to his bitch.

He was just about to step in the room when he heard the distinctive sound of movement behind him. Jag turned around and Ralph was standing there, staring dead at him with a look of confusion and fear. He was a pudgy Yugoslavian man with balding hair and a rotund belly that peeked through his satin robe. He obviously wasn't expecting company.

Ralph dropped the wineglass he was holding and took off running towards the kitchen. He was more than likely on his way to fetch a knife.

Ralph barely made it out the room before Jag blew a hole through the back of his leg.

PFEW!

The gunshot wasn't loud since he had a silencer attached. The lone bullet tore through Ralph's saphenous vein, causing him to fall face first.

"Please, don't kill me! I'll give you whatever you want!" he cried. "I have m—"

His sentence was cut short after Jag yanked a plastic bag over his head. He then secured it tightly with a long piece of cable wire. Ralph struggled and thrashed about wildly, but it was no use against the powerful 6"4 man.

Grabbing him by the leg, Jag dragged him through his home towards the sliding glass doors leading to the back of the house.

Ralph clawed at his neck as the cable wire strangled him to death. He couldn't breathe.

Jag yanked open the doors and lugged him to the modern pool. There was no sympathy in his cold, black heart when he tossed him inside.

Ralph's body hit the water with a hard splash. He immediately plummeted to the bottom like a bag of bricks. He flailed about wildly in the crystal blue water. Either he'd choke, drown, or bleed to the death. Regardless of whichever way he exited, Jag's job was done. The funds were already in his account.

Jag slowly walked back inside the house, leaving Ralph to his own fate. As he walked past the kitchen, he noticed a bottle of Armand de Brignac resting on the countertop.

"Well, hello there. This must be for me."

Jag made a brief detour to pour a glass of $3000 wine. He then found himself moseying through the luxury home in curiosity. Original paintings covered the egg-white walls and the decorative pieces were all high-end. Ralph's ass had some money.

But ironically, the person who paid Jag didn't want that. They just wanted him dead, murdered in the worst possible way imaginable. Jag tried his best to be creative.

Jag's search led him upstairs to the main bedroom. The minute he pushed the door open, he saw a half-naked man lying in bed.

"Who the fuck are you?! RALPH!" he called out.

Jag lifted his gun. Now that he'd seen his face he had to go.

POP!

POP!

Jag canceled his Christmas before he even could realize what was going on. Jag didn't even know Ralph had a visitor. The poor guy was simply at the right place at the wrong time.

On his way out the room, Jag noticed a beautiful diamond ring on the dresser. Next to it was an old photo of Ralph and his wife. She had paid Jag twenty bones to murk her husband after he left her for a man.

Jag thought about abandoning the piece of jewelry. But he figured it could be put to better use than collecting dust, so he grabbed that along with Ralph's wallet.

Cameron will love this, he convinced himself. It completely flew over his head that she hated his guts and everything he stood for. There was nothing he could do or say to redeem his actions. Cam was through with his ass, but he just wouldn't accept that they were over. Their likelihood for marital bliss was very slim.

Jag completely overlooked their problems though. He didn't see anything wrong with the savage way he treated her. In fact, he felt like he was pretty much training her to love him all over again.

After business was handled, Jag went to the hottest strip club in

Reno, *Key Club*. He spent two grand in tips, bought a couple bottles, finessed the baddest stripper into leaving with him, and took her back to his room to beat her out.

The next morning, Jag caught the first thing back to Atlanta. Now that his job was done, he had no reason to stay in Nevada other than to spend money and trick.

The flight back to Georgia was short and comfy in first class. One of the attendants flirted with him the entire time. She had a weakness for handsome guys with dark features and dreamy eyes. Jag reminded her of Christian Grey—only he was fifty shades of crazy. If she knew how dangerous he was she would've ran instead of smiling and making advances at him.

Jag didn't pay her any mind. Once the plane landed Cameron was all he could think about. In all good conscience, he never felt right cheating on her with any of the bitches in the city they lived in. He only dipped his dick in other hoes while traveling, and only because he felt like it came with the territory.

Jag left his family mentality at home whenever he went to do an assignment. Whatever happened during the interval happened.

After exiting the aircraft, Jag headed to ground transportation. He started to flag down a taxi when he noticed a familiar face panhandling nearby.

Was it...? No... Couldn't be...

Jag had to be hallucinating. That was the only explanation he could think of. But when they made eye contact and she gave a crooked smile, he knew it was real.

It took Cameron all of fourteen hours to unlock the handcuffs using the paperclip she found. She never knew how grueling breaking loose could be until she tried it. It was the toughest thing she'd ever had to do in her life.

Cam found herself having to rest every few hours when she got a crook in her neck or overexerted her muscles.

It was 10 a.m. by the time she finally broke free. Pale sunlight spilled through the window into the spacious room. It was a beautiful day out, but a place of absolute torment inside the log cabin. Why couldn't Jag just let her live her life peacefully? Why did he have to go all Jack Torrance on her? There was no explanation for his rapacious nature. One day he'd just snapped, and shit was never the same since.

Cameron never anticipated for things to come to this. Thinking the grass was greener on the other side had landed her with a certified psycho.

After jumping out the bed, Cam ran to the door, and eagerly twisted the knob. She'd almost forgotten that Jag locked her inside. "HELP!" she screamed. "*Heeeeelp!*" Cameron knew the cabin was secluded but it was still worth a shot. Someone could've been nearby hunting in the woods. Maybe they'd hear her screaming and call the police. *I've gotta get the hell outta here*, she told herself repeatedly. "Justin!" Cam called out. "Justin, can you hear me?!"

If Cameron got his attention, maybe she could get him to unlock the door. When he didn't answer she became hysterical and started banging on the surface wildly.

Cameron ran around the bedroom, looking for something she could use to escape. Frantic, she rushed to the nightstand and pulled open the top drawer. Inside was an assortment of wallets. Cam quickly flipped through each one of them. It took her a second to realize they belonged to Jag's victims. His twisted ass kept every single one, like some weird collector's hobby. They were his glorified trophies.

Cam saw their faces on their IDs and felt pity for every one of them, no matter the reason they had to be gunned down.

After grabbing a random Visa, she ran to the door, and dropped to her knees. Sliding the plastic card in between the door, she bent it the opposite way, forcing the lock to go back.

The door popped open almost instantly.

Cameron wasted no time running through the cabin to look for her children. She was almost to their bedroom when Rebecca literally thwarted her path. Before she could open her mouth to say something, Cam checked her ass.

"You didn't fucking hear me screaming in there?! Are you fucking deaf or something? You should've called the police!"

"I don't want to be in the middle of something I know nothing about."

Cameron was mortified by her discourteous answer. In anger, she pushed the shit out of her. "Then move, bitch! Get the fuck out my way! I should smack yo' stupid ass!" She went in the children's room, and found them both tucked comfortably in their cribs. Cam was just about to grab Journee when Rebecca boldly stopped her.

"I'm sorry, but I can't let you take them. I don't think he'll like that at all."

Cameron cut her eyes at the oblivious woman. "*He?*" she repeated. "Bitch, do you even know who *he* is?"

"I don't care who *he* is. *He* paid me $2,000 to watch his damn kids and that's exactly what the hell I'm gonna d—"

Cameron punched her ass dead in the mouth. She was tired of her flapping her gums. Rebecca dropped to the floor and cradled her split lip. She never saw it coming. Any other time, Cam would've felt bad, but considering the circumstances she felt liberated.

"You deserved that shit and more! Be glad I don't stomp a hole in yo' mothafucking ass! You sat here all fucking night, listening to me scream for help, and didn't do a damn thing! I *should* fuck you up, bitch!"

Rebecca cowered in fear, and it wasn't until then that Cam realized she was being unnecessarily violent. Jag's ways must've been rubbing off on her.

Turning her attention away from the frightened babysitter, Cameron focused on her children. By then, both of them were wide-awake and alert. Cam bundled Journee up tightly in her blankets and then took Justin by the hand.

"Give me your phone and car keys," she told Rebecca.

"P—please...I don't want any trouble. I don't wanna be in the middle of anything! I—I met him in a bar the other day. I don't even know the guy," she cried, believing infidelity was the real issue.

Cameron was disgusted that Jag wasn't better acquainted with Rebecca. He didn't know her background, and yet he had her watching their kids. What the fuck was wrong with him? Who would do something so careless?

"I said give me your mothafucking phone and keys! Don't make me ask again!"

Rebecca scrambled to her feet and retrieved the items. With trembling fingers she handed them over. Jag's baby mama had her shook.

Cameron snatched them out of her hand and quickly left the cabin as if it were engulfed in flames. She shivered a bit at the rush of cool air that greeted her. Cam felt no remorse for taking the innocent woman's PT Cruiser. That bitch could rot in hell for all she cared.

After securing the kids in the car, she hopped in the front seat and started the engine. Thankfully, there was enough gas in the tank to get far away from the cabin as possible.

Cam's heart pounded with fear as she pulled out the driveway. She didn't even know where she was going. She had no GPS, no sense of direction, and was virtually surrounded by forest and wildlife. All she knew was that she needed to put distance between her and that god-awful cabin.

In the rearview mirror, she saw Rebecca run out, cursing at her. Blood painted the Hollister sweater she wore. Her lip was still leaking.

I bet her ass never steps to a mother sideways again. Cameron had made sure she learned her lesson.

Slamming her foot down on the accelerator, Cam peeled off, burning rubber. She was so close to freedom that she could taste it—

BOOM!

Out of nowhere, a sedan slammed directly into the side of the retro styled compact car. Cameron's head smacked the driver's window, causing her to immediately lose consciousness. Fate had just dealt a terrible blow. Her plan to escape was purposely sabotaged.

Billows of smoke expelled from the hood of the Cruiser. She

barely made it out the driveway before the collision occurred. Justin and Journee hollered in the backseat of the car. The excitement and danger was too much for them to handle.

Journee had actually fallen under the passenger seat after the crash. Her tiny face was red and puffy as she hollered at the top of her lungs. She should've been in a car seat, but Cam was so set on getting away that she overlooked it.

Jag took his time climbing out the sedan. A second person hopped out his passenger seat. He had come home earlier than planned only to catch Cam trying to escape yet again. She was relentless...and predictable.

"I don't know when this silly ass bitch is gonna learn," he said, shaking his head. There was a strained expression on his face. He was tired of her useless attempts to run. Cameron belonged to him and he was unwilling to compromise.

Jag opened the Cruiser's driver door and glass spilled out onto his black Balenciaga sneakers. There was a tiny cut on the side of Cameron's head. Her body was slumped in the seat. She looked dead, but he knew she was only knocked out.

Rebecca ran up, pulling her hair out, and acting frantic that her vehicle was totaled. "My car! What the hell?! My fucking car!"

"How did this happen?" Jag asked, angrily.

"It wasn't my fault! She just took off!" Rebecca scrutinized the damage to her vehicle. "I don't even have insurance! What the fuck is wrong with you people? Are you gonna pay for this shit?"

"No," Jag said. "You are." Without warning, he grabbed his gun, and blew her fucking brains out. She dropped to the pavement on the side of the street like a sack of potatoes. There was a dime-sized hole in her cranium emitting a thin haze of smoke.

The loud sound of the gunshot echoed, making the children cry even harder. Luckily for him, the nearest neighbor was miles away, and people hunted nearby regularly. No one would suspect a thing, and no one would call the police.

After tucking his gun in the waistline of his jeans, Jag fetched the babies from the damaged car and took them back inside the cabin.

When he came back out Cameron was slowly coming to. She looked up at him with slightly blurred eyes. She couldn't tell if she was dreaming or not.

Jag barely gave her time to recuperate before sideswiping her ass back to sleep. Tossing Cam's limp, unconscious body over his shoulder he carried her back inside their home. Try as she might, there was no escaping his web of insanity.

6

Cameron drifted in and out of consciousness as she fought to return to reality. When she finally opened her eyes, she saw Jag hanging over her like a dark cloud with a crooked smile on his face. At first, she thought she'd died in the car accident and gone straight to hell.

Damn. I know I did some fucked up shit in life but hell though? That seems rather crass.

"You made me kill that bitch," he said. "I didn't wanna do it but you made me. I couldn't have her ass running to the police so I did what I had to... But her blood is on *your* hands, Cam. I hope you know that shit."

Her eyes darted nervously around the room. She wanted to shrivel up and die after noticing she was back in their bed hand-cuffed. Fourteen hours of lock picking was unquestionably in vain. She was right where she started, miserable, hopeless, and condemned. Tears welled up in Cameron's eyes.

This shit is unreal, she thought.

"How long are you gonna do this?" he asked. "How long you gon' run before you realize no one's gonna love you more than me?"

"Jag, I just wanna go home," she cried. Her voice was huskier than normal due to the tears that were backed up in her throat.

"Home is with me," he said.

"Jag, please—"

"*Ssh. Ssh.*" He placed a finger to her cracked, dry lips, silencing her. "Don't talk, just relax. You hit your head pretty hard." He withheld the fact that he knocked her lights out too. "I have a surprise for you," he said. "Guess who I ran into today at the airport?"

As if on cue, a familiar face suddenly walked in and Cam's entire body stiffened. She didn't think it was possible for shit to get any crazier until now. Yeah, she had to be in hell. That was the only excuse for what she was currently seeing.

There was an awkward pause in the room.

For months, Jag talked to thin air, believing it was his sister...but now Alessia was actually standing there in the flesh. "Auntie Lessie's home," he said happily.

After Anzia was murdered, Alessia hitchhiked from Savannah back to Atlanta. Jag was always traveling for work, so she was never able to get in touch with him. She tried calling, but all his old numbers were disconnected.

When he moved to Ohio last year to be with Cam he was far beyond her reach by then. Jag was a killer so his tracks were always covered, making him tough to trail. He didn't keep the same numbers, he never stayed in the same place long, and he moved around a lot.

Alessia was torn up about her mom and too scared to return home at first. But when she realized she needed money she worked up the courage to go back. There was a little cash left over for emergencies, but nothing to survive on. It wasn't long before her homeless downward spiral began.

Since she was an immigrant living in America, Alessia wasn't a societal concern. No one reported her missing. No herd of people came looking for her. She had no family, no friends in Savannah. For over a year she lived on the streets and took care of herself. She survived by begging for spare change and sleeping in abandoned buildings. More recently she began soliciting donations at the airport. That was where she fatefully bumped into her brother.

Alessia had been on the run, homeless and alone all that time. And she blamed everything—including her mother and brother's death—on Cameron. Jag may've wanted to keep her alive, but she had secret intentions of torturing her to death. As soon as he turned his back, her ass belonged to Alessia.

None of this is real, Cam told herself. She closed her eyes tight and prayed she eventually woke up. *Maybe I hit my head harder than I thought and I'm still unconscious.*

When she opened her eyes again and saw the 17-year old glowering, she realized none of it was a dream. Jag's sister looked at Cameron handcuffed to the bed and smiled wickedly. There was a demonic, homicidal look in her dark eyes.

JUICY CARRIED her shopping bags across the *Beachwood Mall* parking lot. Since spending Wayne's cash was her favorite pastime, she decided to pick out a few pieces at the mall. She was nearly at her car when she heard a female's voice behind her.

"You feel good about yourself?"

Startled, Juicy accidentally dropped her car keys. As a stripper, she was used to bitches coming for her over their men. It wasn't her fault they chose fun over faithfulness. Juicy just knew a fight was about to pop off in the lot. She turned around, ready to brawl, and met the penetrating stare of an aggrieved wife.

"You feel good about yourself trying to break up a happy home?" she repeated.

Juicy tuned her aggression all the way down after recognizing the angry woman. "Tabitha..." The name left her lips in a low, inaudible whisper.

Wayne's wife scoffed and shook her head. She had her two children with her. Wayne's lying ass had told Juicy they were teenagers and practically out of the house, but they looked no older than three and four. The youngest held a colored sponge ball in his hands. They both stared up at Juicy with innocent, wistful eyes that asked, "*Why are you taking our daddy away?*"

Juicy felt a tiny shred of guilt—but it disappeared as soon as Tabitha opened her mouth again.

"And the bitch knows exactly who I am. How ironic?" she said. Tabitha approached Juicy thinking she didn't know what she looked like, but clearly that wasn't the case.

"Look, I ain't trying to go there with you. And besides, if it were such a happy home, you wouldn't be standing here wasting your breath talking to me. You'd be with his ass—"

"I can't be when there are whores like you eating off my plate!" Tabitha peeped the shopping bags in Juicy's hands. She knew her husband was the reason why she had them. "Your trashy ass needs to crawl back and *stay* in whatever gutter he found you in. I'll be damned if I share my husband with some filthy, tatted up street-walker. So tell me...how much is it gonna cost to make you disappear?"

Tabitha reached in her Louis Vuitton purse for her checkbook.

Juicy looked as if she'd never been so offended in her life. She used to shake her ass nightly for tips, but something about the way Tabitha offered the cash was flat out rude. "Outta respect for your kids being here, I'm not gonna slap your ass."

"Stop tearing us apart, dammit!" Tabitha screamed. Her voice quivered with emotion as tears filled her eyes.

Juicy knew right then that everything Wayne told her was a lie. Tabitha didn't look like a woman who was close to divorcing. She was desperately in love with her husband and determined to keep her family together. Juicy was nothing more than a trespasser, a sidepiece.

Juicy quickly grabbed her keys off the ground. She didn't know what else to say. All she could do was flee in embarrassment. She would check Wayne's ass later.

After unlocking her door, Juicy opened it to climb in—but Tabitha slammed it shut.

"You will *never* have real love! Bitches like you only get a taste of what that's like by stepping on another woman's toes! Your story never ends well, sweetie. You can bet your ass that you gotdamn home wrecker."

"Lady, you better back the fuck up off me before your kids witness you get your ass whooped. You don't want them mothafucking problems now. Trust me."

In the midst of Juicy and Tabitha arguing, the youngest accidentally dropped his sponge ball. It rolled several feet away in the parking lot, and he excitedly ran to retrieve it. Unfortunately, he didn't notice the Yukon Denali coming straight at him.

SCCCCCCCRRRRRRRRRR!

BOOM!

"NOOOOOOOOOOOO!"

7

"I have to fly down to Miami for a day to handle some business. I'm gonna need for you to be on your best behavior," Jag said.

Alessia looked at her brother from the sofa with an attitude. Her dark sandy brown hair clung to her face. There was a tiny splash of freckles across her nose and cheeks. She hadn't changed clothes or showered since she arrived. She showed a complete lack of refinement.

A putrid odor seeped from her pores, but she'd grown used to her own filth. Her hair was wild, dirty, and desperately needed grooming. Alessia looked, smelled, and acted like a problem child, but Jag was so happy to have her back that he accepted her the way she was. For over a year he had thought she was dead. Alessia could've been blind, deaf, and dumb, as long as she was alive and breathing.

When Jude told him he didn't kill her, Jag didn't believe it. He almost didn't believe she was actually real either until she ran up and hugged him. Now that they were reunited, all hell was going to break loose. Those responsible would eventually pay.

"*Be on my best behavior?*" Alessia repeated, skeptically. He was berating her like she was still a child. "As in don't invite boys over or as in don't kill your girlfriend?" Sarcasm dripped from her tone. With her tattered clothes and unkempt hair, she looked like she lived in the damn jungle.

Jag pulled on a leather Saint Laurent biker jacket. He knew it would take some time for her to adapt to the real world again. "Both," he said with a serious expression.

Alessia grimaced. She felt a chill of disapproval in the air. Jag telling her not to kill Cam was like a parent telling a kid not to eat candy. The temptation was beyond inviting.

"I mean it," he said, noticing her hesitance. She had that crazy Campioni look in her eyes. She was up to no good.

"I know you do," she said in Italian. "I promise I won't go near the bedroom." Alessia held her dirty palms up in mock surrender. Cam would've lost it if she knew those same hands would be tending to her children while he was gone.

Jag walked in the bedroom and smiled at Cameron. There was a grim look on her face. She was miserable.

"Someone else needs their trash taken out, so I gotta split for a day—"

"Don't leave me here with her! She does not fuck with me! You can't see that shit? Please don't tell me you're that fucking oblivious," Cam said, making her opinion known. Her eyes pleaded for him to reconsider. She could look at Alessia and see the hostility. Cam wasn't stupid. His sister despised her, and he knew that shit. Maybe this was his way of punishing her for trying to run.

Jag smiled reassuringly. "I talked to her. You'll be fine."

"Please, Jag, no. I don't want her around my kids—"

"Stop fucking calling them *your* gotdamn kids! They're my fucking kids too!" He paused. "Well, one of 'em at least."

"Jag, I'm begging you—"

He rudely cut her off since he wasn't trying to hear it. "See you tomorrow."

Jag walked out of the bedroom and past Alessia.

"I'm outta here."

"*Arrivederci,*" she sang innocently.

As soon as the front door closed behind him, Alessia wiped the phony smile off her face. She looked at the bedroom door that was currently shielding Cameron from her death. She then heard the sound of his car pull out the driveway.

Jag would be gone 24 hours. More than enough time to have some fun with Cameron.

"I won't kill the bitch... But I'll damn sure make her wish she was dead."

Cameron was staring up at the wood ceiling when Alessia opened the door and walked in. Evidently, she wasn't the only one who knew how to pick a lock.

Cameron knew there was tension between them, but she still begged for help. "Please get me out of here! You have to help me! Call the police!"

Alessia looked surprised and amused. She smothered a laugh at Cam's silly statement. "Why in the hell would I wanna do anything for *you*?" she asked. "I wouldn't spit on your black ass if you were on fire. I'm certainly not gonna *help* you. I would rather die."

Cameron found her comment rather harsh. "Look, Alessia, I don't know what Jag told you, but...He needs help. Professional help." A tear rolled down her cheek after reliving everything Jag put her through. The abuse, the forced sex, and the seclusion—it was all too much.

Alessia slowly strolled over to the bed. She had a growing hatred for Jag's girlfriend. "Are you calling my brother crazy?"

Cameron shook her head vehemently. It was obvious there was no getting through to the teenager. "Alessia, please—"

"The only thing crazy he's ever done was love you." Her mouth tightened. "Honestly, I don't even know what he sees in you. You're *not* even that pretty if you ask me."

"Alessia, why are you doing this? I've never done anything to you," Cam cried.

"*You've never done anything to me?*" she laughed. "Did you just say you've never done anything to me? Is that really what you believe?" Alessia was clearly offended by her declaration. Alessia noticed the paper clip lying on the night table. She picked it up and slowly approached Cam. Her eyes were filled with lunacy. "Don't pull that guiltless shit with me, bitch. Jag might think you're innocent and worthy, but you aren't shit. You'll never be shit...and neither will your children."

"Get the fuck away from me, lil' bitch! I don't wanna hurt you but I will!" Cameron warned her.

Alessia laughed at the meaningless threat. The fact that Cameron was handcuffed to the bed and still thought she was dangerous was flat out comical. She couldn't do a damn thing but sit and sulk.

"You already killed my mother and brother. There's nothing more you can do to hurt me," she said, animosity brewing in her tone.

"Wh—what? I didn't even know your mother was dead! Jag told me that—"

"Shut up!"

Whap!

Alessia slapped the shit out Cameron so hard that her ear rang afterwards. The younger girl was more heavy-handed than she thought.

"Alessia, stop, you don't have to d—"

Whap!

She smacked Cam again in the face, this time leaving behind a red handprint. Then she hit her again, and again, and again. Drunk on power, the 17-year old slapped and clawed at Cam's face like she was possessed.

One of Alessia's fingernails scratched the surface of her eye, and Cam screamed out in pain. The young bitch had lost her mothafucking mind wailing on her.

After seeing the damage she caused, Alessia smiled devilishly. Revenge was sweet, even if she had to deal with her brother's backlash later on. Alessia grew up in a family of contract killers, so she doubtlessly had a few screws loose.

There was a deranged look on her face as she held the sharp end of the paperclip over Cameron's left eye socket.

"Don't you fucking dare! Get that mothafucking thing out my

face!" Cameron tried to turn away, but Alessia grabbed her cheeks, and forced her head still.

The teenage girl really got a sick thrill out of torturing the bound woman. Jag told her that Cam was strictly off limits, but she just couldn't control herself. Someone needed to pay for her relatives' murders. Why not Cameron?

All of a sudden, Journee started crying in the other room. She was in an irritable state and needed attention. She also might've saved Cam's life too, because Alessia stopped just seconds before puncturing her eye.

"Sounds like the mongrel baby needs me." She grinned mischievously. "Duty calls."

Her racist comment made Cameron believe she might hurt her children. "Don't you touch my fucking kids, you young bitch! I swear to God I'll kill yo' mothafucking ass if you touch 'em!"

Alessia ignored Cam and skipped delightedly out the room before closing the door behind her. That little heathen was worst than *The Children of the Corn*. She was the devil reincarnated.

Cameron listened to Alessia soothe the infant, surprisingly getting her to calm down. She breathed a shaky sigh of relief, thankful that she didn't hurt her. With the way Alessia was talking, Cam didn't know what to expect. After all, her beef was with her. Not the children. *Maybe she isn't as crazy as I thought.*

Cameron devoutly hoped it was true.

All of a sudden, she heard a loud thump followed by Justin crying.

"Shut up! Shut the fuck up!" Alessia screamed.

Evidently, she was wrong in her assumption.

"What are you in there doing to him?!" Cameron yelled from inside the room. "What the fuck are you doing to my son?!"

In horror, she listened to what sounded like slapping and tussling. Justin's high-pitched cries grew louder and louder. Alessia brutally assaulted the toddler, since she knew that would hurt Cam more than anything.

"GET AWAY FROM HIM, YOU BITCH!" Cameron screamed

from the bedroom. Her heart started beating so fast she could feel it in her throat. "Leave him the fuck alone!" Her voice was hoarse with rage as she fought to free herself from the cuffs. Unfortunately, no safety pin was nearby this time. It pained her that she couldn't even see what Alessia was doing to him. There wasn't shit Cam could do but listen to her son cry and call out for her. "LEAVE HIM ALONE!"

8

J ag pulled into the driveway of his secluded cabin home and smiled. He was $20,000 richer, his sister was back, and his family was finally unified. Life looked promising.

After turning off the engine, he walked in the house, and found his sister sleeping on the sofa. It was eight in the morning, so he considered cooking breakfast. Leaning down, Jag planted a soft kiss on her forehead.

He then went in the bedroom, where he was greeted with the sight of bloodstained sheets. Cam's wrists were cut and bruised from hours of trying to break free.

"Cameron?" Jag took slow, cautious steps towards her. His stomach clenched into a little knot. Her head was dipped low, and he couldn't tell if she was breathing or not. "Damn. What the hell did you do to yourself?" He knelt down beside her and placed his ear next to her lips to see if she was breathing. He didn't hear anything. His first thought was that she'd committed suicide. "Shit." Jag put his burner on the night table, pulled out his keys and un-cuffed her. Cam's body dropped limply onto the bed. He was almost certain she was dead. He felt a wave of relief after detecting a heartbeat. "Cameron? Cam, get up, baby."

Suddenly, her eyes shot open, and she kicked the shit out of Jag, sending him flying out the bed. Cam saw the gun lying on the nightstand and quickly grabbed it.

Scrambling to her feet, she pointed the pistol down at Jag without remorse. He sat up on his knees in prayer fashion and stared at Cam with pitiful eyes. His ass really fell for the okie-doke.

"So that's it?" he asked. A smile tugged at the corner of his lips. "You just gon' shoot me? Like that? After everything we've been through? I killed for you," he reminded her.

"You killed for *you*," she corrected him.

There was a twinkle of amusement in his eyes. She could hear just the faintest hint of laughter in his tone. He didn't think she really had what it took to pull the trigger.

Cameron gave him second thoughts after cocking the gun. Her finger rested on the trigger. Tears rose to her eyes and spilled over her lower lids. She hated his ass with every fiber of her being. She didn't know how she could've ever loved him.

Jag soft blue eyes darted back and forth between Cameron and the gun. He had a relaxed disposition despite staring down the barrel. "Give me that before you hurt yourself, girl. It's not like you really gon' shoot m—"

POP!

Cam shot his ass in the head at point blank range. Regret didn't exist as she watched his body land with a thud.

After hearing the gunshot, Alessia frantically ran in the room to see what happened. She took one look at her brother sprawled out on the floor and lost it.

"OH MY GOD! What did you do?! What did you fucking do! You fucking bitch!" she charged at Cam full speed and was clocked by the gun.

Alessia dropped right next to Jag's body, and Cam quickly climbed on top of her. Gripped by rage, she pistol-whipped the teen with every ounce of anger she had in her soul.

WHAP!

WHAP!

WHAP!

WHAP!

By the time Cameron finally exhausted herself, Alessia was barely recognizable. Her face was a swollen, bloody, distorted mess. But she didn't get anything she didn't already have coming.

Cameron climbed off Alessia's semi-conscious body, grabbed Jag's car keys, and went to get her kids. This time she moved much more quickly and efficiently. When she saw the welts and bruises on Justin's body, she felt like killing Alessia. The gun trembled in her hand. She had every reason to go back in the bedroom and empty the clip. Instead of doing just that, Cam hastily whisked her children to the car.

After safely securing them, she jumped in, and started the engine. She was just about to pull off until she remembered she was in the middle of nowhere. She would need a phone for navigational directions and possibly to call the police.

Cameron grabbed the gun out of the passenger seat, climbed out the car, and went back inside the cabin. Her heart pounded as she got closer and closer to the bedroom. She half-expected one of them to be gone, like in the scary movies but was thankful they were right where she left them.

Alessia groaned in pain. Surely she'd never had a worse beating in all her life. At least now she'd think twice before putting her hands on somebody else's child.

Cameron stepped over her body and knelt down beside Jag. Regardless of everything he put her through, she did feel somewhat bad for killing him. There was once a time when they were best friends before becoming lovers. Things quickly took a turn for the worse. He got abusive, psychotic, and ended up on the receiving end of a bullet.

Cam tried not to look at the pool of blood spilling from his head as she reached for his jeans. She slowly dug the iPhone out his pocket and stood to her feet.

All of a sudden, Alessia grabbed her leg.

Cameron jumped in surprise.

"...I'm gonna bury your ass, bitch—"

WHAM!

Cameron kicked her hard in the face, immediately knocking her out. She and Jag deserved to rot in hell together. Now that Cam had what she needed, she ran out of the cabin and jumped in the car. She couldn't get away from that dreadful place fast enough.

9

It was 4 p.m. on a Wednesday, and Jude was drowning his sorrows like the alcoholic he'd become. A small hole in the wall bar down in Old Fourth Ward District was his sanctuary from society. Normally, Jude kept a few shooters with him, but lately he'd been careless about his safety and well-being. He migrated alone like he didn't have a slew of enemies waiting to catch him slipping. It was almost as if he had a death wish.

Jude tossed the shot of scotch back and slammed the empty glass on the counter. He wheezed dramatically after the liquor burned his throat just a little.

"You want another?" the bartender asked. He was a tall, dark-skinned cat with a box fade and part line. He was also a member in Jude's intricate car theft ring. On his off days, he stole cars to later on be shipped overseas and sold at a higher value.

Jude was making a killing off his business until Jag came and fucked everything up. He was a pain in his ass, like a damn hemorrhoid that needed to be dealt with.

Jude placed a C-note on the counter and stood to his feet. "Nah, I'm finna gon' head and slide. I'mma get up wit'chu though."

"Aight then, man. And thanks for the baby shower presents. My girl ain't stopped fawning over 'em since she opened 'em."

"Aw, c'mon now. You fam. You already know how I do," Jude told him. He treated his niggas like they were blood. They were all closer to him than his own relatives—especially after losing his mom and older brother, Jerrell.

Jude dapped his homie and left the bar, pretending he was sober enough to get behind the wheel.

"You know your fine ass shouldn't be driving," a random female boldly spoke up. "You ought to let us chaperone you." She was standing outside with her girl smoking a cigarette. They'd both peeped the illustrious young boss the moment he walked out.

Jude was dapper that evening in a black Moschino button down, fitted designer jeans, and Prada sneakers. Two gold Cuban link chains dangled around his tattooed neck. The latest addition was his wife's name.

Jude's clothes and swag echoed his general demeanor. The fact that he didn't have a bitch on his arm gave them the impression he was a free agent.

If Jude felt that way, he would've fucked Essence last night when he had the chance...but he didn't. Instead, he walked in the bar, took one look at her and left before she noticed him. While she did look inviting in a crop top, black booty shorts, and mesh stocking, she wouldn't have filled the emptiness in his heart. The only useful thing she could do was help him get a quick nut off. Afterwards, he would feel terrible and regretful. Not only that but Essence wasn't Cameron.

No one could take her place, and no one could fill the void he was missing without her. Anytime he looked at a woman, all he could see was Cam's face. He couldn't go on living like this.

Jude surprised himself by nearly chuckling. "I'll manage," he said.

The girls pouted in disappointment, mad they couldn't make a quick come up off him. Jude wasn't that nigga. He was older now, smarter, and wiser. He didn't have time for the bullshit.

It took him less than 20 minutes to get home. When he pulled his

'Rari into the circular stone driveway, he noticed an unfamiliar car parked in front of the fountain.

Jude never got around to fixing the lousy security system, and he wasn't surprised that someone just let him or herself in. Jude immediately grabbed his thumper and climbed out the Italian sports car. He had a bullet for any mothafucka feeling foolhardy.

"Who the fuck is this?"

As soon as Cameron saw Jude she stepped out of the car. Ironically, she had just pulled in less than two minutes earlier.

Jude thought he was drunk and imagining shit after he saw his wife standing several feet away. There was dry, smeared blood on her face from when Jag slapped her around. Her hair was a mess. But as certain as death and taxes were, there she was plain as day.

Jude looked no better. His dreads were past due to be re-twisted and he could've used a lineup. He needed someone to take care of him and vice versa.

Jude and Cam ran up to each other at the same time and hugged tightly. He had to touch, and hold, and kiss her just to make sure she was real. They say sometimes people needed to fall apart to realize how much they needed to fall back together. Perhaps that was true in their instant.

"I been missing you like crazy. You have no fuckin' idea, yo."

"I missed you too." She cried tears of joy.

"God brought you back to me. I ain't ever lettin' yo' ass go again, Cam," he said, reassuringly. "I love you so much."

"I love you too."

Jude was so wrapped up in his family that he didn't notice his phone vibrating in his pocket. It was Magyc calling to let him know that Roxie had finally woken up from her coma.

10

Three Months Later

Cameron and Roxie were seated at a table in Starbucks inside *Lenox Square Mall.* They were childless that afternoon since their men had given them a break for once. A few shopping bags sat near their feet as they filled each other in on the latest tea in their lives.

Despite the conspicuous scarring left from Jag's attack, Roxie looked healthy and like her old self. The weight that she'd lost in the hospital was put back on in just a few short weeks. In an effort to start a new beginning, she hacked off all of her pretty hair. Now she wore it in a short finger wave style. Someone else may've not been able to pull it off but Roxie slayed. It was especially cute since she had a fine grade of baby hairs.

She was sexy and sleek that day in a white jumpsuit and leather jacket. Her makeup was minimal, aside from the dark red MAC covering her lips. Although she was fully healed and looked good, Roxie felt the exact opposite inside. Lately, she and Magyc weren't on the same page, and it had a lot to do with his cheating ways.

"Something's changed," she said. "I just don't know what

happened to all promises he made when I was in the hospital. He swore that he wouldn't fuck up again. He claimed he was gonna change, and that he was gonna marry me. I may have been in a coma but I heard every single thing he ever said to me. And I believed every word like a damn fool."

Cameron saw the stress and mental pressure their relationship was putting on Roxie.

"His ass hasn't kept a single promise," she complained. "I don't know who's worst. Him for putting on or me for staying."

"Don't blame yourself. Besides, you know how niggas are. They always wanna *change* when it's convenient for them." Cameron made air quotes at the word 'change.' "And it sad too because I really thought he'd do right by you. He definitely made it seem that way when you were down and out."

"Girl, that hoe ass nigga ain't done right by nobody but himself. He deserves a fucking Oscar. Talk and action are two different things, and he's failing miserably with one. I should've stopped dealing with him when I found out he was still seeing Briana," she said. Flash-backs of his ex showing up at her apartment came to mind. She shuddered inside when she pictured Jag blowing her head off. Roxie quickly shook the painful memories away. She attended counseling sessions regularly just to help her cope with the traumatic incident. "All that good shit Magyc was popping off was just game. I'm finally starting to see it now."

Roxie felt like she was still being punished for sleeping with her sister's man. Ever since she fucked Calix it seemed like every relation-ship she got in was cursed. O' Zone was murdered in a nightclub, her baby daddy died in a tragic car accident, and now Magyc was shitting all over her heart.

Cameron opened her mouth to respond, but snapped it shut when she saw a familiar face in the crowd of people. Roxie watched all the color flush from Cam's face. Her eyes were round with fear. She looked like she'd saw a ghost.

"What is it?" Roxie asked, turning in her seat.

A dark-haired white guy walked past with his girlfriend.

"I thought that was..." Cameron's voice trailed off. She didn't even want to speak his name. "Never mind," she quickly said. When Cam looked back at Roxie she could read criticism in the sharpness of her gaze.

"Cam, you do this shit every time we go out. You realize that, right? You gotta break free of the chains," she said. "Stop torturing yourself and move on. That mothafucka is dead."

Cameron sighed and took a sip of her iced coffee. Roxie was right. She had to stop agonizing over the past. "C'mon. Help me find a top to wear," she said, desperately changing the subject. "Jude wants to take me out this weekend."

"Alright now," Roxie smiled. "You ain't said nothing but a word. I can definitely help get you together." She took immense pride in her creative fashion sense.

Together, they started their hunt for the perfect shirt. Trailing close behind them was one of Jude's bodyguards. He was 6"4, 230 lbs. of solid muscle, and the first to shoot when shit popped off. Jude wouldn't let Cam leave the house without some form of protection.

She and Roxie had just walked out of *BeBe* empty-handed when Jude Face Timed Cam.

"Wassup, babe?" she answered.

"You. I'm missing yo' ass already," he said.

Cameron smiled and blushed like they were interacting for the very first time. Something about him did that to her. She loved everything about her husband. His gentle brown eyes, his beautiful thick, fuzzy dreads, and his lips that weren't too big and weren't too small. Every single thing about him made her heart beat just a little faster. She was given a man that was everything she dreamed of and everything she needed. The answer to her prayers.

"I'll be home soon," Cam told him.

"Don't stay out too late," he said, rather bossily.

She bit her lip and then forced her mouth into a smile. "I promise I won't. Let me say to hi to the kids real quick."

Jude moved the camera so that she could see Journee and Justin. "Say hi to mommy."

Her son grabbed the phone excitedly, and put it so close to his face that she could see up his tiny nostrils. "Hi mommy," he sang.

"Justin, move the camera back. I can't see you," she giggled.

While, Cam talked and laughed with her family, Roxie noticed a group of fine ass men walk past. There were maybe six or seven of them, and they all possessed an air of confidence.

The most attractive of them was a young Korean guy with jet-black hair and near perfect features. He was so damn cute that Roxie had to do an automatic double take.

He had smooth ivory skin, a slender button nose, small kissable lips, a cut in his left brow, and dark hooded eyes that were seductive by default. He was a pretty boy, but possessed a bohemian street style that was the complete opposite.

His ensemble consisted of a gray beanie, which covered half his head, a long sleeve cream top, destroyed jeans, suede boots, and a plaid shirt wrapped around his waist. His jewelry was minimal, but not a single piece cost less than $10,000. There was an enigmatic aura that surrounded him. His confident stride matched that of an acclaimed celebrity. He had an instinctive sense of propriety about himself.

Roxie saw Asian men all the time in Atlanta—especially in Midtown. But she knew right away that he wasn't from the A. He didn't look like he was from Georgia, period.

All of a sudden, he made eye contact with Roxie and smiled. It wasn't an intensely flirtatious smile—just one that conveyed the mutual attraction.

She shyly smiled back. Something about the way he looked at her made her feel tingly all over. But she forgot that sensation in an instant when she remembered that she had a boyfriend. And he damn sure wouldn't have approved of her gawking at some other dude. No matter how suave and good-looking he was.

Magyc better get on his shit, she thought. *There's plenty other men who would jump at the opportunity to take his place.*

11

"**M**an, ain't nobody takin' my girl's place so get off that sucka shit," Magyc told Tara. "I'm tired of havin' this mothafuckin' conversation wit'cho ass. Every time I come through you on the same ole' bullshit."

Tara was his ex-girlfriend, Briana's best friend. Back when she was with Magyc, they used to have threesomes all the time. Unbeknownst to Briana, their affair continued outside the bedroom and well into his second relationship.

Magyc knew he was dead wrong for stepping out on Roxie, but a nigga was going to be a nigga at the end of the day. He had no real aspirations of ever seriously settling down.

In the beginning, he tried to do right by Roxie, but over time he eventually went back to his old, whorish ways. Nearly losing the love of his life just wasn't enough to correct his flaws.

"How is me wanting to be a priority bullshit?" Tara asked with an attitude. She was completely naked in bed with the sheets bunched around her bosom. They had just finished fucking, but you wouldn't have known it based on Magyc's hostility. As usual, he was giving her the runaround.

Magyc deliberately avoided her eyes. "'Cuz you know my bitch ain't havin' that shit. Fuck you talkin' 'bout?" he snapped.

Tara pursed her lips and resisted the urge to slap him. His answer wasn't a sufficient enough explanation. "She wouldn't be able to handle a lot of shit if she really knew the truth."

Magyc didn't like the sound of that at all. As a matter of fact, it sounded like a blatant threat. "She ain't *gonna* fuckin' know," he said with finality.

Tara watched as he secured the gold straps on his Giuseppe sneakers. Afterwards, he pulled his Givenchy tee shirt on. Magyc blew thousands on clothes, cars, jewelry, and strippers but tossed her a meager $5,000 a month.

"She won't unless I tell her..."

Suddenly, he yoked Tara up by her throat. "Don't fuck with me, T! I'm tellin' you, the last thing you wanna do is fuck with me!" he threatened. "Chill out with all that bullshit! You ain't finna say shit. Not if you want me to keep droppin' this dick in yo' back."

"Nigga, fuck yo' mediocre ass dick! Get your gotdamn hands off me!" Tara pushed him. "If you want me to continue keeping this shit on the hush then I'mma need more than just five punk ass bands."

"That's what'chu trippin' on? Some mothafuckin' money?" Digging in his pocket, he pulled out a knot and threw the cash at her like she was a prostitute. "Here! Take the fucking money, bitch! I ain't trippin' on this lil' shit!"

Magyc started to leave, but Tara quickly jumped out the bed and went after him. "It's about more than just the money, Magyc!" she finally admitted.

Without warning, he turned around and shook her violently. "You all over the mothafuckin' place! Get the fuck off my back, Tara! GOTDAMN!" He threw her onto the mattress and left the bedroom angrily. He was so easy to upset, and she wondered if it was because his drug usage had increased.

Tara was putting unnecessary pressure on him, and he didn't need that shit now. She knew he had a bitch. She'd known for the last year, and now she wanted to act up.

This mothafucka something else, he told himself. Tara had good pussy—some of the best out there—but she wasn't worth the fucking headache.

When Magyc reached the living room, he saw her three-year old son watching TV on the couch. He more than likely heard them arguing, but it wouldn't be anything new for him.

Magyc walked over and hi-fived him. "Wassup, lil' man. You good?"

"Yes..."

"What's this weird ass shit you watchin', yo'?" He wasn't the most experienced when it came it came to dealing with children. Shit was so much easier with Rain because she couldn't talk.

"The Octonauts," he said jovially.

"Fuck is that about?"

"Underwater animals..."

For a three-year old, Marlon was very smart and perceptive. Magyc wouldn't have been surprised if he knew how crazy his mama was.

Tara and her son lived in a nice two-bedroom apartment in Home Park. Magyc paid her whopping $2500 rent, and yet she acted like he never did shit for her. However, he knew that finances weren't the real issue. She wanted something more from him. Something he just wasn't ready for.

Two seconds later Tara burst out the bedroom wearing a silk robe. Dark purple marks had already formed on her neck from him choking her. "You ain't shit, Magyc! You ain't fucking shit! You're worse than worthless! I don't even know why I deal with you! All you do is walk over me! I swear I'mma just stop opening my door and legs for yo' ass! I'm tired of dealing with a nigga that ain't gon' change!" She was near tears as she outlined his many faults.

Magyc was completely unfazed by her meaningless threat. He had easy access to both her home and pussy whenever he wanted. And there was never a time when he worried about another man being there. Last time she tried that shit, he broke her company's nose and sent his ass to the hospital. It was no secret that Magyc had a fucked up temper. It didn't help either that he was also the jealous type.

"Do what'chu gotta do," he said nonchalantly. And he meant that shit too.

"Oh believe me, I will. Starting with putting your mothafucking ass on child support..." she said with resolution.

Magyc was halfway to the door when she hit him with that shit. Her unexpected threat immediately caused him to stop in mid-step.

"Damn, so you gon' pull that card on a nigga?" he asked.

"I'm tired of you treating us like we're your secret! You run all around the city with that bitch, claiming her daughter like she's yours, but don't do a damn thing for your own son!" she pointed out. "What type of fucked up shit is that?"

"Bitch, I ain't even want the lil' m—" Magyc caught himself just before he said something hurtful in front of the child. At such an early age, he was already very impressionable. The last thing Magyc wanted was Marlon thinking that he hated him. It wasn't like that at all.

When Magyc was seventeen, Tara got knocked up while they were fooling around. Briana, of course, had no clue and he simply wanted to brush the pregnancy under the rug. After all, he wasn't ready for kids. He damn sure wasn't trying to father a side bitch's baby.

Magyc paid Tara to get the abortion, but she did what the fuck she wanted to. He never wanted a kid with her ass, but she was so determined to start a family even with lacking moral support.

Tara's mother died from cancer at an early age and her pops was nowhere in the picture. That was partly the reason she wanted her own family so bad. She got tired of being lonely. The only people in her life were Briana, Marlon, Magyc, and a few other close friends.

After Briana died, she felt emptiness. Though Tara was fucking her man, she still considered Briana to be the closest thing she had to a sister. Things just happened between her and Magyc.

After burying their friend, she and Magyc started spending even more time together. Despair and vulnerability had pushed them right back into the arms of each other. Tara didn't understand why she couldn't leave him alone. Magyc wasn't shit. He knew it. She knew it. Hell, Marlon even knew it.

Magyc didn't take care of his kid, he hardly spent any time with her, and he did nothing to make her feel special. Yet every time he popped up, she opened her door to him with open arms.

Magyc was worse than any drug she'd ever experimented with. She knew the harm he'd inflict, but she just couldn't stay away.

"I ain't 'bout to do this with you. Besides, you just talkin' out the side of yo' neck. I know yo' ass ain't crazy." He headed to the door with poise and confidence. Something told him Tara was just blowing smoke as usual. "Hit me when you out yo' feelings, aight?"

"She gon' leave yo' stupid ass 'cuz you don't give a fuck about nobody but yourself, Magyc!"

Once the door closed behind him, the tears started flowing down. Tara hated herself for allowing Magyc to use and abuse her. It wasn't fair that he flaunted Roxie and Rain, but treated her and Marlon like crap. They were there first—before the hoes, money, and street fame.

If this nigga really thinks I'mma keep taking his shit he has another thing coming. Tara knew where he and that bitch lived. And since he refused to take responsibility, she planned on broadcasting the truth herself.

12

Car ain't got no roof...
        Car ain't got no roof...
        We be in da city...
All my bitches with it...

Young Dro's latest club banger thumped through the speakers inside Persuasions Gentlemen's Club. They'd just recently recovered from a shooting that occurred nearly two years ago and was back up and running.

It was the same place Cameron danced at when she first moved to Georgia. In fact, it was Cam who recommended the club to Juicy after she relocated to Atlanta. There was a relatively thick crowd that night with a roster of over thirty girls. Persuasions had upgraded tremendously since reopening.

The classy upscale establishment now featured two bars on either side of the club, a brand new catwalk stage for the strippers, and high-end VIP suites. Shutting down and starting fresh was just what they needed to come back better than ever.

In the dressing room, Juicy sat at the vanity and stared at her fatigued reflection. Her conscience was heavy after Tabitha's son was hit and killed in the parking lot that fateful afternoon.

Juicy was so grief-stricken by the death that she packed up and left her hometown the very next day. She didn't even talk to Wayne about the whole ordeal. She just fled, desperate to escape the guilt.

Juicy felt like his loss was all her fault. If she wasn't fucking a married man, Tabitha wouldn't have confronted her in the parking lot, and their son wouldn't have died.

Juicy was devastated. There were even moments when she contemplated suicide, but she never went through with it. Instead, she tried her best to pick up the pieces and move on.

In an effort to leave the past behind, Juicy blocked Wayne's number, and avoided him at all costs. She didn't want to be found. She didn't want to be bothered. And most importantly, she didn't want to deal with her problems face to face.

Juicy peeled her eyes away from the mirror and proceeded to get dressed. She was a slave to the stripping lifestyle. Since she dropped out of high school and didn't have a GED, her occupational choices were thin.

Juicy had been dancing since the tender age of eighteen and she was hooked on it. The fast cash was addictive like the strongest drug. Every time she hit the stage in her six-inch heels it was like taking a hit.

"Bitch, you always looking like a sad ass puppy every time you come in this mothafucka," Dynasty teased. She was a cute Puerto-Rican chick with green eyes and a diamond-shaped face. Her ass was entirely too big for her petite legs, but the niggas all loved it.

"I be having shit on my mind," Juicy said.

Dynasty approached her at the vanity. She'd just gotten off stage and she was still topless. Her pink nipples were double pierced and she had a sun tattooed around one. Juicy had never seen anything so bizarre until she met Dynasty. She was also one of the top money-makers in the club.

"Do a drop with me then?" Dynasty offered. She could tell Juicy needed something to take the edge off.

"Fuck it. Why the hell not?"

Dynasty went to her locker, unlocked the combination, and

pulled a tiny clear bag out her purse. That bitch had so many different color tabs you would've thought she was the Connect.

Juicy graciously took one straight with no chaser. She tried to stay away from liquor since it made her rather aggressive. She hadn't popped a cap in years, but right about now it may've been just what her nerves needed.

Fifteen minutes later, Juicy emerged from the dressing room feeling exhilarated. She looked sultry in a pink and black two-piece with rhinestones. Instead of the shaved hairstyle she normally sported, she now rocked a shoulder length bob.

Juicy entered the main club in high spirits thanks to a little MDMA boost. She planned on making some money tonight. Rent was due soon, and she needed a new set of wheels. Juicy had left her precious BMW back in her hometown. She couldn't risk taking it along and Wayne reporting it missing. She didn't need those problems. Besides, Juicy wouldn't have been surprised if he hated her ass. He probably felt the same way she did, like it was all her fault. If she weren't arguing with Tabitha, then she wouldn't have taken her eyes off her son.

Juicy shook the thoughts off as she sashayed through the club. She felt every man's eyes on her coke-bottle shape. She was definitely in the top five for Persuasions' hottest dancers.

The timing was perfect since she was next on stage. Every man who was curious about her could finally watch her perform and hopefully show some generosity.

"Aight now fellas! Get'cha mothafuckin' ones ready and welcome my girl Juicy to the stage!" the DJ announced.

Her giant tattooed ass cheeks jiggled as she walked up to the stage. It was all natural, no preservatives.

Fetty Wap's club anthem poured through the subwoofers. Twenty minutes ago, she was depressed but now she had the upbeat energy of a hyperactive child. All eyes were on Juicy as she mounted the stage and grabbed the 15-foot pole.

I'm like, yeah, she's fine...
Wonder when she'll be mine...

She walk past, I press rewind...
To see that ass one more time...
And I got this sewed up...

Juicy bounced, gyrated, and popped to the rhythm until a flurry of bills rained down on her. She really got the crowd's attention by shimmying to the top and flipping upside down. Thanks to her incredible arm strength, she was able to twerk with her ass to the ceiling.

A money shower came shortly after. Juicy slid down into a complete split before riding the stage. While doing her thing, she noticed a tall, cute, chubby light-skinned guy walk in the club. He had a full beard and a boss-like presence that emanated from him.

The moment he strutted inside the strip club all the dancers flocked to him. Every female knew who he was except Juicy. Every piece of jewelry he wore shined superfluously. His style was unique.

Damn, why these bitches so hype though, she wondered. Initially, she thought he was a famous producer or upcoming rapper. He certainly had the body language and self-assurance of one.

A beige crochet Kufi was situated on top of his head. He wore a black Middle Eastern tunic, Balmain jeans, and $500 red suede loafers. Juicy wasn't quite sure what his nationality was. The fact that he left her curious meant she was obviously interested.

Apparently, he felt her staring, because his eyes shifted to the stage. He looked at her with an ambiguous smile and she immediately felt butterflies.

Juicy turned her attention away from him to focus on her crowd of admirers. There was a group or seven or so men huddled around the stage, fanning bills. *I don't know why Cam said she hated stripping down here. It's mothafucking money in the South. That bitch is tripping*, she thought.

Juicy was making her ass bounce to the bass when her admirer walked up with a knot. He threw a fat stack of singles on stage, outshining every fella that tipped her.

She winked at him. He smiled, and then swaggered off to the bar to get a drink.

Juicy cleaned up during her turn, and when she descended, men were eagerly at her neck. They either wanted her number or to talk her ear off about nothing. She bypassed all of them to thank the man who really had her attention.

The bitches had finally given him some breathing room, and he was now solo at the bar, sipping a Red Bull. When Juicy reached him, she awarded him a hug that he gladly accepted. He gave her booty a gentle squeeze while doing so. He wanted to make sure that motha-fucka wasn't hard like half the bitches walking around. He liked a soft ass. Not that pumped up, steroidal shit.

"Damn. You put all ya groupies on hold for me? Gotta nigga feelin' flattered now and shit." There was a hint of humor in his tone. His eyes twinkled with amusement.

"You know I had to come and thank you for showing me love," she said.

Juicy tried her best not to stare too hard. He was even sexier up close in person. His emerald green eyes captivated her. He had bushy brows that almost kissed, but a beautiful texture of hair. She could tell from his plush beard and the part of his head that wasn't covered by the Kufi.

A shimmery diamond grill coated his fronts, the Rolex on his wrist sparkled brightly, and he smelled of Tom Ford Tobacco Vanille. Everything about him screamed money, and yet he was low-key at the same time. From his swag, to his demeanor, to his looks, he was all the way on point. His ass was too damn fine.

Damn, I see why the hoes going crazy, Juicy said to herself.

"Aye, you got it," he told her.

She didn't know it but he'd been an admirer of hers for a couple years now. He saw her movement on IG, and knew she was a legend in the stripper game.

"Can I freshen up and dance for you?" Juicy offered.

He hesitated a little. "Shit, I'on really be on all that when I come through. I'mma have to pass this time, lil' mama."

Juicy gave him a quelling look. "Why not?" she asked.

She was cute and all, but he didn't feel like it was necessary to explain his reasoning. So instead he pointed to a group of nearby overzealous young guys waving ones. "Them the mufuckin' tricks right there," he said. "Go give 'em hell."

Juicy grimaced. "It was nice meeting you."

"Yup..." He never bothered introducing himself, and Juicy walked off somewhat irritated.

She didn't expect his reaction at all. It was almost like he was pushing her on someone else since he didn't want to be bothered. His cocky ass lightweight got under her skin by rubbing her the wrong way. She wasn't used to men turning her away.

Damn, I'm happy we ain't hit it off. No way in hell I'd ever fuck with an arrogant ass nigga like that. Juicy told herself that, but she had no idea the future held a different set of cards.

13

It was sunset when Magyc strolled in he and Roxie's apartment. His ass was MIA for two whole days, and had the nerve to come and try to love up on her. She was in the kitchen cooking when her man stepped behind her and wrapped his arms around her waist.

His firm body pressed against hers. Magyc hit the gym on the regular and it definitely showed in his physique. Roxie felt his erection push against the cleft of her booty. The sight of her in nothing but pajama shorts and a lace camisole had him harder than a bitch. Half her ass was hanging out the bottom of the shorts.

"Damn, girl. You been walkin' 'round the house in this shit all day?" he breathed in her ear. "Gotdamn...You was waitin' for me to drop this dick in you, huh?" Magyc tried to kiss her neck, but she turned away.

"You really think you gon' get some pussy after going AWOL?"

"*AWOL*? Man, I been out my bustin' ass, handlin' business. If I'm always here then I'm broke. You love this lifestyle, don't you?"

"Don't hit me with that bullshit. You don't be out handling business and you know it."

"Girl, stop cuttin' up and lemme shove. You know you need some dick. That's why yo' ass actin' crazy now."

"No, I'm acting crazy 'cuz I got a nigga that pretends he don't see his phone ringing when I call."

Magyc squeezed on her ass while rubbing his dick against her. "I told you I be hustlin', girl. Stop givin' me grief, yo'."

"Move, Magyc. I ain't really in the mood."

Frustrated that she wasn't turned on, he finally backed off irritably. "Man, yo' ass ain't never in the mothafuckin' mood. Few weeks ago you was on yo' period. Couple days ago you ain't wanna fuck 'cuz we ain't have no jimmy. Now you ain't in the damn mood." He shook his head. "You got more fuckin' excuses than a bitch on prom night."

Roxie turned around so fast that specks of hot grease flew off the spatula she was holding and onto his shirt. He felt a few tiny drops burn his face, but luckily none got in his eyes.

In the face of extreme pain, Magyc remained collected. He prided himself on his absolute calm, because truthfully, he wanted to fuck her up.

"And have you ever asked yourself why?!" she yelled.

"Why what? Why you makin' me strap up all of a sudden? You used to let me smack out raw all the time. What changed?"

"*What changed*? Are you seriously asking me that? You've changed! How could you not see it?" she asked him. "You are *not* the same man I fell in love with! I feel like I don't even know you anymore."

"Damn... So you don't even know me now?" He seemed genuinely disappointed to hear that.

"That's right. I don't know you and I don't trust you," she said with validation.

His eyes widened in disbelief. "*Wooowwwww!* You don't trust me? How the fuck could you not trust me?" he asked, loftily.

"Because I don't!" she yelled, defiantly. "I don't trust you with my body. I don't trust you with my heart. I don't even trust you with my life."

"Man, you talkin' crazy right fuckin' now. Where all this shit even comin' from?"

"Nigga, it's coming from months of pent up frustration!" she yelled. "You haven't done any of the things you promised me! You haven't changed! You haven't stopped fucking around!" Tears snaked down her cheeks as she confronted him. He was finally dealing with the consequences of a woman who had bottled up her emotions for far too long. "What happened to all that shit you said about getting married? Huh? What happened to you promising me you'd be a better man?"

Magyc was ruefully silent.

Roxie ran her tongue along her inner cheek while shaking her head. "Funny. You got so much shit to say when you're making empty promises. Now all of a sudden the cat got your fucking tongue."

"Man, get the fuck outta here with that. I'm just not 'bout to sit here and argue with you 'bout some shit that ain't true."

Roxie propped her hands on her curvy hips. "So you *haven't* been fucking around?" she challenged.

Magyc studied her in her moment of acrimony. She was a gorgeous girl with a cherubic face, doll-like doe eyes, wispy lashes, and pouty lips. Her skin was the color of melted cocoa. He absolutely loved dark-skinned women. Chocolate was his favorite flavor.

Roxie was perfect for him.

Damn. Then why do I keep fuckin' up, Magyc asked himself.

He wanted to be faithful and treasure her like she deserved...but he'd damned if he didn't fuck other hoes. A young, flashy nigga with paper, bitches threw pussy at him on the regular. He couldn't help that he was constantly faced with temptation. Or so that was how he thought.

Instead of telling Roxie the truth, he stood right in her face and lied. "No I haven't."

She gave him a doubtful look. "So you been one-hundred percent faithful and devoted since I got out the hospital?"

"I don't know how to be no other way."

"See? That right there is why yo' nose so gotdamn big. You lie too fuckin' much."

"How am I lying? Don't pin some shit on me you can't prove, bruh." He preferred speculation to admitting his wrongs. If she didn't have sufficient evidence then he would continue to plead the 5.

Roxie folded her arms and looked at him like he'd said something sideways. "A couple weeks ago the toilet was clogged up. You were out running the streets—doing only God knows what—so I had maintenance come take a look at it," she said.

"And?"

"*And* there were condom wrappers backed up in the mothafucking pipes."

Magyc hurried to a conclusion. "You actin' like we don't wear condoms now. I must've flushed 'em by mistake."

"They were Lifestyle! Not Trojans! I've never fucked with that cheap shit. That means you had another bitch in my house... Probably even more than one! Who knows? There ain't never no fucking telling with your trifling ass."

This was Roxie's first time telling him about the condom incident. Just reliving it again made her want to slam the scorching hot frying pan on his head. Having another female in her house, in her bed was just flat out blasphemous. She should've left his ass then, but she didn't.

It had gotten to the point where she was simply staying with him so that she wouldn't be lonely. Roxie felt safe when he was around, although rare. He comforted her when she had night terrors about the day Jag attacked her. He was good with her daughter, Rain. But it just wasn't enough. She needed commitment and she needed a man who wouldn't disrespect her.

"Magyc...I...I can't do this with you. I think we may need some time apart," she finally said.

Magyc looked crushed by her words. He had actually never considered the possibility of her leaving him. Hearing her say that quickly made him retract. He couldn't lose her. Not now. Not like this.

Magyc grabbed her waist and pulled her close. "C'mere, yo'. What'chu mean you can't do this? What'chu sayin'?" he asked, calmly.

"I have to stop selling myself short. I deserve more."

"You could never sell yourself short with a nigga like me."

"Magyc, I—"

His only thought was to kiss her into silence. "I don't wanna argue with you. I don't wanna fight wit'chu. And I damn sho'll don't wanna lose you. On some real shit, you the best fuckin' thing that's ever happened to me." He then blamed their tension on his absence. "I'mma do better. I'mma start spendin' more time with you. I'm done fuckin' off in the streets. From now on when I get through workin' I'm comin' straight home to you. You're my first concern," he stressed. "Nothin' or nobody else. And I'm sorry if I gave you the impression that you couldn't depend on me. You're every fuckin' thing to me, Rox. I never wanna make you feel that way."

Lies fell from his lips, but there was unwavering love in his eyes. Roxie knew he was probably blowing smoke, but still allowed herself to believe him. Looking up at him with a sweet earnest expression, her heart melted. Roxie was a slave to his love. He had a death grip on her heart.

Magyc pulled Roxie closer to him and held her. He knew he had to treat her better if he didn't want to lose her. It was rare that he found women like Roxie. She was a novelty. He couldn't squander a good thing. The bond he and Roxie shared was incomparable. He would never find that nowhere else.

"Let me make it up to you...right now," he added. "Lemme take you out somewhere. Anywhere. You decide."

Roxie started to remind him that she was cooking, but realized she'd unintentionally burnt the ground beef for the pasta. She was so caught up in the heat of the argument that she didn't smell the smoke.

Magyc turned the stove off for her and took the spatula from her hand. "Gimme this and you go get dressed," he said. He just wouldn't accept her leaving him. He had to pull all the stops to make her stay. Roxie was the real deal, and Magyc knew it'd be tough finding another girl like her. Someone that put up with his shit and adored him endlessly despite his many flaws. No one in the world loved him more than Roxie.

At first, she was apprehensive about accepting his offer. After all, she was just trying to break up with his ass two minute ago. But, as always, Magyc lured her back in with false hopes and empty promises.

"Okay," she murmured, hesitantly giving in.

Roxie turned to leave, but he grabbed her wrist, and pulled her towards him. "You know I'd do anything to keep you happy, right?"

Her face was unreadable. "I hope so..."

Magyc lifted her hand to his lips and kissed the back of it. "From here on out, I swear I'mma do better by you. Just watch. I'mma remind ya ass why you fell in love with a nigga in the first place."

His statement relieved a small amount of doubt, but he had a bad habit of not keeping his word.

"Only time and actions will show and prove," she said.

14

Magyc told Roxie to pick anywhere she wanted him to treat her. She had hundreds of choices, but she settled on a four-star oyster bar in the west end of Midtown.

When Magyc pulled his Lamborghini Roadster in front of *The Optimist* valet quickly rushed to get their doors. Roxie stepped out in a threaded blue Chanel blazer, a white $900 Alaïa skirt, and silver sparking Louboutin Pigalles. A white Chanel bag accentuated the outfit perfectly.

Roxie made sure to cover her scars with foundation prior to stepping out. Her confidence level just wasn't the same now that she had them. And it didn't help that Magyc cheated on her with strippers, video vixens, and models.

Deep down inside, Roxie felt like he wasn't attracted to her anymore. Sometimes she wondered if he merely stuck around because he pitied her. She was a single mom who had recently survived a devastating attack. Maybe he felt partly responsible for what Jag did, so he stayed out of obligation.

Magyc laid to rest her lack of faith when he took her hand and walked inside the restaurant. When she looked up at him he smiled, offering a warm sense of comfort.

Perhaps he really does want to change, Roxie convinced herself. Maybe there was promise for them after all. She prayed there was, because as much shit as she talked she didn't want to be without him either.

It was extremely crowded that evening in the restaurant. There was even a waiting line just to eat inside. Luckily, they were seated quite promptly thanks to the generous tip Magyc slid the host.

He was dressed to the nines in a cream long sleeve crewneck sweater, fitted forest green cargo pants, and black Burberry military boots. His dreads were pulled back and secured with a rubber band. The Audemars watch on his wrist cost more than the average car. As always, he was fresher than a newborn baby.

Their outfits were in sync to some extent. People marveled at the fact that they were a cute couple. If only they knew of the bullshit they went through behind closed doors.

Roxie tried her best to put their problems behind her. Tonight was all about focusing on how they could make their relationship thrive.

The waitress that came and greeted them was a young, cheerful, pecan-colored chick with a bubble butt. Normally, Roxie never felt insecure when they were publicly out somewhere. Magyc usually did everything he could to make her feel certain of herself—but that was before the "incident".

Roxie's confidence level instantly shriveled up when he and the waitress started smiling flirtatiously at each other. She was supposed to be speaking to both of them as she recited her spill, but she couldn't stop ogling Magyc.

This ratchet, fucked up weave-wearing, indentured ass servant is really 'bout to bring the hood out of me, Roxie thought.

The girl was hardly even cute, but she doubted Magyc cared. She knew that he was an ass man.

When the big booty waitress sauntered off to get their drinks Roxie went in on him. "Damn. I was afraid if you stared any harder you might strain something."

Magyc sucked his teeth and sighed. "Man, what'chu goin' on about now?" He was irritated that she was about to start some shit.

"Nigga, what do you think? I'm blind? I had PRK done three years ago," she reminded him. "You were gawking at that bitch like she was the main entrée—"

"Lower yo' damn voice," he warned.

"I'm not lowering shit, nigga. How 'bout you stop lowering your fucking standards!"

"Man, wasn't nobody lookin' at that bitch—"

"Bullshit. You were eye fucking her like I didn't even exist!"

"That's your insecurities talkin'," he said.

"And if it is whose fault is that?"

Magyc fell silent. Shortly after, the waitress returned with their drinks. She purposely slammed Roxie's cup so hard that water sloshed onto the table.

"Oh, I'm sorry," she said in a syrupy sweet voice.

Roxie mugged the shit out of her ass. She was literally two seconds away from making her lose her job.

Magyc tried his hardest not to look when she bent over dramatically to wipe up the mess. She was fucking with him, and he knew it. Roxie knew it too, and she damn sure didn't look happy about it.

After cleaning the small mess, she took their orders and scurried back to the kitchen. At that point, Roxie no longer had an appetite. Magyc could see the irritation all in her expression and disposition. She was in a sour mood after the waitress' petty antics.

Reaching over, he placed his hand on top of hers. She tensed up instantly but didn't move away. "Now we been through too much for you to be actin' like this tonight. We came here to make peace. Not war."

Roxie relaxed a little, but her heart didn't feel any lighter.

"Get off that shit. You the only girl in my head and in my heart," he said. "The only one that matter."

Roxie forced a smug smile. Sometimes she just needed that tiny ounce of reassurance.

All of a sudden, his phone chimed, indicating a text. Roxie watched him unlock it, look at something that was sent to him, and smile.

Just as easily as she felt reassurance it disappeared. "What is it?" she asked with an attitude. She had a feeling it was some bullshit.

"It's nothin'," he quickly said. Magyc made a move to put his phone away, but she quickly reached across the table and snatched it. What she saw made her want to die from pure mortification.

The damn waitress had sent a naked shower selfie to Magyc. Soapsuds covered her bare breasts and her fingers were in her shaved pussy. Roxie was disgusted. "Are you fucking serious?" she yelled. "This desperate ass cry for attention! I can't believe you got the nerve to be amused by this shit! It's fucking pathetic and so are you!"

"Man, gimme my shit," he demanded.

Roxie ignored him and scrolled up to find various text messages to and from the waitress. He'd been fucking with her all while she was in the hospital, and even after she was discharged. Magyc had met her in the strip club she danced at on the weekends. Roxie had no idea she was the one who'd been giving him lifts whenever he was bent. They shared a history that she knew nothing about until tonight.

"YOU AIN'T SHIT! Here take this mothafucka!" Roxie jumped up and threw his phone at him, causing his drink to spill in his lap. "You can shove it up your ass too while you at it!"

Magyc quickly hopped out his wet seat and grabbed a napkin. The crotch of his jeans was soaked in water, making him look like he pissed himself. "Gotdamn, girl—what the fuck!" he snapped.

Magyc didn't expect her to go from zero to one hundred. It wasn't his fault the bitch was choosing.

Everyone stopped to spectate their wretched behavior. They were in a classy four-star restaurant carrying on like a couple of damn kids. It was childish and beyond embarrassing—but lately Magyc had a tendency of making her act out of character.

By the time he looked up, Roxie was long gone. He was so focused on wiping the water off his pants that he didn't notice her storm out the restaurant. Unfortunately, when he got outside she had already left in an Uber.

Sighing deeply, Magyc ran a hand over his dreads. He was supposed to be making things right between them, but instead he was only digging himself deeper and deeper.

Ten minutes later, Roxie arrived in front of the apartment building they shared. *For once, I hope his ass don't come home,* she told herself. She needed her space from his trifling ass. Time to think if she really wanted to be with a nigga like Magyc. As her man, he was supposed to love and cherish her, but all he did was hurt her. She was tired of putting up with his shit just to retain a permanent spot in his life. It wasn't worth the heartache and pain. She refused to stay with a sorry ass nigga.

Roxie thought about getting a room for a couple days, but refused to have her daughter living out of some hotel. She was still just a baby and didn't fare well with change.

I'm tired of being a fucking fool for this nigga.

On the elevator ride up to her floor, Roxie wiped her tears so that the babysitter wouldn't know she was crying. In all actuality, it really didn't matter. She had left with Magyc and returned alone, so she'd know off rip something happened.

When the elevator doors opened, Roxie heard the unmistakable sound of two women arguing. She started to ignore the catty banter until she heard one mention Magyc's name. That's when Roxie noticed Tara arguing with her babysitter in the doorway of her unit. She was demanding to know where Magyc was since he wasn't answering her calls.

Really? Another mothafucking one? How many hoes does this nigga have?

Suddenly, Roxie noticed that Tara looked somewhat familiar. She favored Joseline from *Love and Hip Hop* a little. It took Roxie a second to remember where exactly she knew her from, and it finally dawned on her that she was Briana's best friend. Tara was the same chick that tried to jump on her during her first date with Magyc.

So this bitch is fucking him now too?

Roxie started to check her ass until she noticed the three-year old boy standing idly beside his mother.

Roxie immediately froze up. He was a spitting damn image of Magyc...

15

The following evening, Cameron, Roxie, and Juicy all met up at *Euro Hookah Lounge* in Buckhead to hangout and chitchat. The massive bar featured high ceilings, elegant red and white tufted furniture, and a regal theme. It wasn't packed with customers, but it was a pretty decent crowd for a Thursday night.

After Juicy moved down to Atlanta, Cameron introduced her to Roxie, and the three of them had been tight ever since.

Cam felt good having real friends by her side to help her heal from the ordeal with Jag. She had a true support system, and she was grateful that she had other people to lean on besides Jude. She loved him to death but there was nothing like having your girls.

Jude was still doing his best to maintain the business, however she noticed that he wasn't as passionate as he was in the beginning when King first bestowed the responsibility upon him. Dealing with Jag and the kidnapping had taken a lot out of Jude. Hell, it had taken a lot out of everyone. Now they were all simply trying to move on and get things back on track.

A tray of Mediterranean finger foods sat on their table along with a tall Shisha, which was positioned in front of them. The women got together regularly to fill each other in on the latest gossip in their lives.

Roxie couldn't wait to dish her dirt about Magyc. She had been starving to tell someone the truth ever since she found out. "Ya'll ain't gon' believe this shit right here. So tell me why yesterday I just found out that Magyc has a side baby."

Juicy broke out laughing hysterically. She was cute in an all black sweater dress and Versace shades. Tall black suede boots covered her shapely legs. "A side baby though? What the fuck is that?"

"The baby of a side bitch. I'mma need you to get hip," she told Juicy. "Anyway, I know for a fact she a side bitch 'cuz she was best friends with Magyc's ex. And if ya'll saw this hoe ya'll would be wondering why he'd even wanna put a baby in her. Ole' horse face bitch. I'm telling ya'll, she has a jawline that'll make you back down in a brawl. Like seriously."

All three women laughed hysterically at Tara's expense.

"Wow! This is all too much..." Cameron said, wiping her tears. "I'm a complete loss for damn words. So you mean to tell me Magyc done fucked around and got a chick pregnant?" She almost couldn't believe what she was hearing.

"Apparently, three years ago..." Roxie said. "The bitch showed up at my door last night going on about how he never does shit for their son—"

"Whoa. Whoa. Whoa. How do you even know the baby is really his?" Cameron asked. "I mean any bitch can pop up claiming their DNAs match. Have you gotten any proof?"

"Yeah, bitch...my eyes," Roxie said, sarcastically. "The little side baby looked just like him."

Juicy howled with laughter. She and Roxie both shared a rather dark sense of humor, which was why they got along off bat.

"Girl, would you stop calling that poor child a side baby," Cam said.

Roxie's lips twisted up. She was only being ugly because she had miscarried his child when Jag attacked her. If she had any sense, she would've been happy she dodged a bullet.

"Have you talked to him?" Cameron asked.

"Hell no. I barely wanna even look at his black ass. He ain't been home since that bullshit in the restaurant. And I couldn't be happier about that."

"What bullshit in the restaurant? Damn. I'm all lost and left in the dark," Juicy laughed.

"You were at work last night. I know you get off late so I ain't wanna blow up with some nonsense," Roxie said. "Anyway Magyc took me out to dinner and was eye raping the waitress the entire time —but that ain't even the worst part of it all. The bitch had the nuts to send a naked selfie *while* we were on our date. Who the fuck does that? Like I swear these hoes have no shame or self-worth."

"Just a bird looking for a quick come up. You already should know these hoes play dirty," Juicy said.

"Are you gonna *try* to talk to him about the baby mama situation?" Cam insisted. "'Cuz this some stuff ya'll really need sit down and discuss. Shit gets real once kids are involved."

"I know... We are gonna have to talk...but... Right now I just been feeling like I need my space, you know? And I'm glad he's respecting that," Roxie said. "I don't even think I could stand looking at him. We not at all where I thought we'd be. It's just been one fucked up thing after the next with him." She'd told them all about the condom incident and his habitual cheating. "All the shit Tara said really got to me. On some real shit, I was so torn up inside that I barely got any sleep."

"*Unh-unh*. Rule number one—never lose sleep over a nigga who's probably somewhere sleeping with another bitch."

Cameron nodded her head in agreement.

"You're right..."

Before Juicy could continue with her lecture, she noticed a familiar person stroll inside the lounge. "Oh my God, Cam," she said in surprise. "Remember the prick from the club I told you about the other day? Funny acting ass light-skinned nigga?"

"Yeah..."

"Well, don't look now but he just walked in."

He was handsome that evening wearing a blue Kufi, silk jacquard shirt, jeans and studded red bottom loafers. The gold Phillip Patek watch on his wrist glistened along with the 18K gold chain around his neck. An Arabic scripture was engraved with diamonds in the pendant. He'd dropped over 20 grand on the chain, so no one could ever question his religion.

On his arm was a beautiful foreign chick with delicate features, dark hair, and plump lips. She reminded Juicy of one of the Kardashians.

Although Cameron was told not to look, she still turned around in her seat. Her curiosity immediately gave them away, and he noticed Juicy instantly. Her stomach flip-flopped when he smiled at her.

Juicy quickly looked away, so that he wouldn't think she was sweating him. Placing his hand on the small of his company's back, he steered her to the rear of the lounge.

"Bitch, I told yo' ass not to look!" she hissed in Cam's ear.

"My fault. It was just an automatic reaction," she giggled. "He's cute though. Not at all how I pictured he'd look."

"Um...can we focus less on Beard Gang and more on my lil' situation at hand? I just found out that Magyc has a whole fucking child for God's sake!" Roxie cried, in a bratty tone. She wanted to vent more about the situation, but it was clear they were no longer interested in hearing about.

"No matter what advice we give it's up to you to decide what you're gonna do. Every week it's something new with him, and yet you choose to stay with his ass," Cam said. "We're not gonna sit here and sugarcoat the shit anymore. And we're not gonna keep telling you he ain't shit. Magyc is my people and all, but there's no sense in continuing to be unhappy. You gotta figure out what's best for Roxie."

After an hour of talking shit and smoking hookah, Juicy excused herself to the little girl's room. On her way out, buddy from the club called out to get her attention.

"You can't speak?"

Juicy stopped and turned to face him. He'd left his companion to come and say hello, but she wasn't too far out of ear range.

"I didn't know you expected me to," Juicy said. She tried to play it off like his olive green eyes didn't make her heart flutter. *Damn.* Why did he have to be so gotdamn handsome?

"You know I wanna see dem lips move as well as dem hips," he said, smoothly. "Plus it'll make my night a lil' better."

Once he reached her Juicy realized how tall he was. There was a commanding presence to him.

"Your night already looks like it's going good," she said, looking over at his date. The young woman seemed totally unfazed that he was all in Juicy's face. Maybe they weren't as serious as she thought. "Who is that anyway? Your girl?"

"Don't worry about who she is..."

"She's looking over here right now so I kinda have to."

"She's a friend," he simply said. "If you want you can introduce yourself. She don't bite." His flirtatious smile implied that she loved women. Ironically, Juicy did too.

"Boy, whatever. You ain't even introduced *yourself* yet. How you gon' just introduce me to somebody else? I don't even know your name."

He held his manicured hand out. "People call me Rico."

She shook it. "I'm Juicy."

"Nah, keep that shit. I want'cha real name."

She smiled bashfully. "Diana."

"Diana what?"

She hesitated a little. "Diana Prince..."

He paused for a second. "I don't know why that name sound mad familiar?"

Juicy scoffed. "Could be 'cuz it's Wonder Woman's alias. My father was a huge comic book fan growing up—"

"That's interesting, but nah, it ain't that," he chuckled. Rico thought about it for a second. "Wait a minute. You from from Cleveland, ain't 'chu?"

Her heart instantly plummeted after his question. She didn't think anyone in the south would recognize her from Cleveland, but she was undoubtedly wrong. "Yeah..."

"Yeah, I thought I knew you from somewhere. You did a party for my boy."

"When?"

"Shit, this was a minute ago. You fuck with T-Dog, right? I wanna say it was downtown."

Juicy lowered her guards after learning they shared a mutual friend. "Yeah, I did. At the Bingham apartments on West 9th, I remember."

It was also the night Cameron was almost raped by Paul in the bathroom. Luckily, Cole came when he did. Juicy had no idea that Rico was there that night. He must didn't stay long. She would've remembered his ass if she saw him.

"How you know T? You from Cleveland?"

"Nah, I just know him from doing business," he said, vaguely.

"Oh ok, cool. Where you from then?"

"I spent a lot of time in New York. But I move around a lot." He then shifted focus. "You go back home and visit often?"

Juicy shuddered inside after the mall incident came to mind. "No, not really..."

"Well, shit I ain't gon' hold you up. I know you got'cha girls waitin' on you. Take down my math and we can chop it later."

"I don't usually date customers." There was a flirty grin on her pretty face. He saw the telltale interest in her eyes despite the bullshit she was spilling.

"I ain't no customer though. I'm that nigga that's gon' add value to yo' life." Rico took her phone and plugged his number in. "Shit, if it ain't beneficial, I wouldn't even press the issue," he said.

"I gotta feeling you trouble," she smiled.

"I might be... But I gotta feelin' you handle trouble well."

A group of guys walking past admired Juicy's plump derrière. They didn't show the slightest consideration that she was talking to another man. She caught them staring at her ass like she was a piece of dessert.

"I promise them lames can't do nothing for you, baby. Hit me up when you ready for a king."

Rico was just about to walk off but Juicy stopped him. "Can I ask a silly question?"

"Wassup?"

"What are you? I'm just curious..."

"*What am I*? I'm a man."

She laughed. "No, I mean like—"

"I'm just fuckin' wit'chu. I know what'chu mean." He chuckled and his green eyes twinkled in amusement. "I'm Moroccan, baby."

Juicy's face lit up with interest and curiosity. She wanted to ask more questions, but he beckoned his company so they could leave. On his way out, Rico tossed a small wad of cash on her friend's table to pay for their meal.

Something told Juicy he was going to be a handful.

16

Cameron teased her hair with a metal rat-tail comb in the bathroom mirror. Normally, she wore it short, but lately she'd been letting it grow out. It reached just a little past her shoulders and was full, natural, and chemical-free.

Cam needed it to lay perfectly this evening. This was she and Jude's first date since only God knew when. It wasn't often they went out together because work always kept him so busy. But for today, Jude had taken the night off just for her. They planned to renew their wedding vows. It wasn't their anniversary. He just wanted to do something simple, special, and romantic to revisit the wonderful day they made it official.

Cam looked beautiful that evening in a white body con dress with cut out sides. She was finally starting to look and feel like her old self again. No more drama, no more madness, and most importantly, no more Jag.

"Hurry up, babe! Our reservation's in half an hour," Jude called out from the bedroom.

"I'm almost ready," she said. Cam quickly dabbed on a little Gucci perfume and rubbed her lips together, which were coated in a matte fire red. She looked fiercely classy.

After making sure her hair was properly styled, Cam left the bathroom and went downstairs to the kitchen. She wanted to pour herself a small glass of red wine in order to get her night started.

Grabbing an empty champagne glass from the cabinet, she padded barefoot to the double-sided sink and turned on the faucet—

KSSSSHHH!

The glass slipped from her hand and shattered when it hit the floor. Cameron froze up after she saw a dark figure standing outside through the kitchen window. *No. No. No. It can't be!*

Panic-stricken, she turned and fled the room, accidentally slicing her foot on a broken shard.

Cameron ran straight into Jude on her way out. He'd sprinted downstairs after gearing the glass break. He already had his chopper in hand, ready to fuck up any intruders.

"It's him!" she cried. "It's him! He's out there! I saw him!"

"Who?"

"JAG! He's outside! I just saw him through the kitchen window! He's here!" Cameron was so livid that she didn't notice the blood pouring from her foot.

"Calm down—"

"Don't tell me to calm down! He's out there, Jude! I have to get the kids!" Jag had her shook. All she could think about was the verbal and physical abuse. She could never go back. Cam tried to run off but Jude grabbed her. She was going to scare the shit out of their baby sitter with all the theatrics.

"Relax. They're safe," he assured her. "You probably just saw the driver. He's been waiting on us for fifteen minutes. That's why I kept telling you to come on."

Cameron shook her head vehemently. "No, it's him! Let me go, Jude! I know what the fuck I saw! It was Jag!"

Jude finally released her and started towards the front door.

Cam's eyes shot open in fear. "Jude, no!"

"If it's him then I gotta bullet with that mothafucka's name on it." He seemed undaunted by the possibility that Jag was outside. Jude knew that son of a bitch was dead. His wife was the only one that had difficulty accepting it.

Cameron fearfully watched as Jude unlocked and opened the front door. Her heart pounded so hard in her chest that she was sure he heard it. Suddenly, she realized she was weaponless. If he were out there, then surely she'd need something to protect herself.

Cameron thought about going upstairs to get her burner until she saw the driver standing outside in front. He was smoking a cigarette and looked relatively annoyed that they'd made him wait so long.

Cameron felt like a total fool. Roxie was right. She really was torturing herself.

Jude turned around and looked at Cameron. His eyes were filled with disappointment and sympathy. "You gotta stop doin' this shit, Cam. It ain't healthy for you. It ain't healthy for me. It ain't healthy for none of us, bay," he stressed. "Sooner or later, you gotta realize that you won't be at peace 'til you let that shit go. You gotta move forward, babe." Jude suddenly noticed the blood on her foot. "Gotdammit Cam," he said, irritated.

Cameron looked down at the cut on her heel. It was pretty bad but not deep enough to require stitches. If it weren't for him acknowledging her injury she would've never noticed it otherwise. Jag had her mind and emotions all over the place.

Jude quickly went to the bathroom to get a first aid kit. When he returned, Cam was trying her best not to stand on her foot.

Jude lifted her bridal style and carried her to the closest chair. After carefully placing her down, he proceeded to dress her wound. "You gotta stop doin' this, Cam," he said again. "It hurts me to see you hurting like this. I hate that I can't take that weight off ya shoulders 'cuz you deserve happiness."

Cameron stared at him with loving eyes. She could see how strongly he cared about her. Jude was right. She had to stop with the antics, because it was only affecting those she loved.

Cameron reached out and gently ran her fingers along his cheek. He was incredibly soft, like baby's skin. Jude affectionately nuzzled her hand, savoring her warm touch. He never wanted to lose her.

"I love you with all my heart—and everything I'm made of, Cam. I'll always protect you and be by your side until my last breath," he promised.

"I know you will...and I love you for that."

He smiled and looked up at her with earnest eyes. "You wanna know somethin' funny? I don't think I ever knew what real love was 'til I met you, Cam. And I never wanna lose that. I'd die before I ever let someone hurt you again."

THIRTY MINUTES after their little dilemma, Jude and Cameron arrived at a newly built restaurant in Virginia Highlands. The neighborhood pub featured classic Italian comfort food, exposed-brick interior, and an outdoor patio in back that faced North Highland Avenue.

When the driver pulled in front of the restaurant and opened the back door to their limo Cam's mouth fell open. "Jude! OH MY GOD! You didn't!" she said excitedly.

Positioned above the entrance doors was a huge sign that read *Cameron's Trattoria.*

They were supposed to be renewing their vows tonight, and he said he had a gift for her. But she had no idea it'd be an actual restaurant. Not only did Jude want to do something sweet for her, he also wanted to invest his money into a legal business since he planned on getting out the game for good. That was a surprise he had yet to reveal.

"I did," he said. "And I did it for you."

"Jude—I—I'm at a loss for words." Tears filled her eyes. She never thought she'd see her name on a sign somewhere. Jude just never ceased to amaze her. He still had yet to show her the new billboard for the establishment.

"That's cool. You don't need words for this." Jude pulled her close and kissed her passionately.

Taking Cameron by the hand, he led her through the newly

constructed restaurant and to the back patio. It wasn't too chilly so she didn't oppose dining outdoors.

Their table was already set up beautifully with silverware, dishes, two candles, and a single red rose for Cam. Ever the gentleman, he pulled out her seat before taking his own.

A bottle of Dom Perignon sat between them and Jude did the honors of popping the cork. He poured them each a generous amount. The flames from the candlelight danced against his golden skin. He was clean-cut and stylish that day in a Hermes three-piece with a white button. His dreads were piled high in a man bun. Her husband was beyond compare.

"Jude, this is beautiful... I love it," Cameron said.

"You and me, girl...Go a long way back..."

Upon hearing someone sing, she turned in her seat and saw instrument players and a man crooning a soulful rendition of Blood-stone's 1982 classic.

"I remember when loving you wasn't easy. It wasn't easy, baby... But I stuck on in there with you... And we made it. Sugar, we made it... Through it all... Now let's keep it up 'cuz I ain't had enough... You and me, girl...Go a long way back..."

Cameron looked over at Jude with tearful eyes of gratitude. There was an impish grin on his handsome face. Reaching over, she placed her hand on top of his. Some men got lazy with their efforts in keeping their woman happy—but not Jude. He just kept finding new ways to love her and show her how much he cared.

"And I know you remember when trying to love me wasn't easy. It wasn't easy, baby... But you stuck on in there with me... And you see, we made it. Just you and me... And we love each other so... Girl, we can't let each other go..."

Cameron was so wrapped up in the performance that she didn't notice Jude place a jewelry box on the table. He tapped her hand to get her attention, and her gaze shifted to the velvet case.

"What is it?" she asked, breathlessly.

"Open it..."

Cameron took her time lifting the lid. Her eyes instantly lit up at the three stone emerald diamond ring. Cam's original one was tossed out by Jag in a jealous fit of rage.

"Oh my God, Jude. You didn't have to do this, baby."

"I wanted to," he insisted. The new ring was expressly for reaffirmation. He needed Cam to know he was just as committed to their marriage, as he was the day he asked her to be his wife.

"Jude, I...it's...absolutely remarkable. Thank you, baby."

Just then a waiter stepped out onto the patio with a basket of fresh bread. Before he could place it on their table, a slug whizzed past and shattered the bottle of champagne.

Glass exploded everywhere as more bullets came sailing towards them.

POP!

POP!

POP!

17

Cameron screamed and ducked for cover. A peaceful ceremony was suddenly impeded with gunfire. She almost thought she was trapped in a nightmare until she saw the waiter struck down by a bullet. His blood splattered all over Cameron's face and expensive dress.

"Get down!" Jude yelled, snatching his burner out.

Two of his men rushed outside after hearing the chaos. One of them was kind enough to whisk the band away from danger.

As Cameron dropped to the ground she noticed a teenage girl coming right their way with a loaded Ruger.

POP!

POP!

POP!

Alessia was hell-bent on avenging her family as she emptied her clip. She would've clap backed sooner, but she had her hands full trying to locate Cam. And thanks to Jude, she did. He'd bought a billboard in the city to advertise his new business, and as fate would have it, Cam's face was right at the bottom. Alessia's prayers had finally been answered. And now that she had Cameron in her sights, she planned on finishing what she started back at the cabin.

That bitch should've killed me when she had the chance, Alessia thought. *Now she was in for a rude awakening.*

Dressed in all black from her skullcap to her shoes no one ever saw the 17-year old coming. She looked just like the contract killers that raised her and taught her how to be a cold-blooded murderer.

Jude quickly flipped their table over to use as a shield. A hollow point hit one of his boys, but he didn't have time to see if he was okay. Jude was too busy trying to protect his wife from harm.

POP!

POP!

Jude left off two shots of his own—and Cam quickly ran over to stop him. "NO! Don't kill her! She's just a kid!"

Jude violently snatched his arm from his wife. "I DON'T GIVE A FUCK! This lil' mothafucka shootin' at us! You don't think I'mma lay dis young bitch down?!" Swinging his arm over the edge of the table, he fired off a few more rounds.

POP!

POP!

POP!

Cameron was in the middle of an all out war. As much as she hated Alessia's crazy ass, she didn't want her to get hurt. She was a disgruntled teen with a chip on her shoulder, but she didn't deserve to die. At least not in Cameron's eyes.

In an effort to make the shooting cease, she jumped up and yelled, "*STOOOPPPP!*"

"Cameron, no! What the fuck are you doing?!" Jude yelled from the ground.

Alessia took one look at Cam and pointed her gun—

"Enough is enough! It's over! It's all over, Alessia! Just stop! Enough people have suffered already. You don't have to do this!" she pleaded.

Tears poured down the young girl's cheeks. "Yes, I do! I have to! 'Cuz the person who should've suffered the most hasn't!" she yelled. Alessia didn't care how insane she looked opening fire in the heart of a busy commercial district. She didn't care about the innocent lives at stake or the consequences of her actions. If she died tonight, she planned on taking Cameron down with her. "Don't you get it?" she asked. "I *have* to do this!"

"Cameron!"

"NO—"

POP!

A single bullet ripped through Cameron's body, sending her falling backwards. Jude caught her just before she hit the ground. His first reaction was to shoot until he ran out of ammo.

POP!

POP!

POP!

Holding his motionless wife in one hand, he opened fire on Alessia with the other. Once his chamber emptied, he tossed the gun, and centered his attention on Cameron. She wasn't moving, and he couldn't tell if she was breathing. Tears clouded his vision as he searched for where she'd been hit.

Jude's men continued to shoot at Alessia, but their bullets hit everything in sight but her. Car windows exploded, tires flattened, and a nearby restaurant's window was shot out.

Alessia wanted to annihilate them all, but her ammo was on E. Quickly taking off on foot, she ran in the opposite direction. She could hear the faint resonance of sirens wailing, and didn't want to be around when the police came—

BOOM!

Out of nowhere, a moving vehicle accidentally slammed into Alessia. The gun flew out of her hand, and she slid off the hood, and crashed into the ground.

The frantic, uninsured driver sped off in haste, desperate to flee the scene of the crime. The only reason he was driving recklessly to begin with was because he'd heard gunshots.

After a grueling struggle, Alessia miraculously stood with no broken bones and minimal bruises. Unfortunately, that was where her luck ended.

Several patrol cars surrounded Alessia before she could escape.

She thought about trying her luck anyway until the cops hopped out and drew their weapons.

"Freeze!"

"Don't move!"

"Get down on the ground!"

Red and blue sirens lit up the dark street. They had the entire corner blocked off. Frightened citizens watched from the windows of their homes and establishments like they were staring at a suspenseful episode of *Law & Order*.

Alessia shielded her eyes from the bright light coming from above. When she looked up, she noticed a Fox News helicopter hovering in the sky. The eager reporters fought to get the perfect angle of her possibly being gunned down.

"I said get on the fucking ground! NOW!"

Alessia refocused her attention on the angry policemen. They all looked ready to open fire at a moment's notice.

Damn.

It really *was* over.

There was nowhere to run, nowhere to hide, and no one to have her back.

With nothing left to lose, Alessia leapt for her gun on the ground —but was tackled from behind by a cop. She fell face first on the concrete, busting her nose wide open.

Thankfully, someone got to her before they had to light her young ass up. They didn't want to shoot an adolescent, but they would've if they had to.

After being roughly snatched to her feet, Alessia was handcuffed and read her Miranda rights. "You have the right to remain silent. Anything you say or do can be held against you in the court of law. You have the right to an attorney. If you can't afford one, then one will be appointed to you."

From her peripheral, she noticed Cameron being tended to by medical personnel.

The bitch is alive?

EMTs placed Cam onto a stretcher, covered her face with an

oxygen mask, and wheeled her off to a nearby ambulance. Jude was by her side the entire time. He'd been grazed on his arm by one of the bullets, but it wasn't shit a few stitches couldn't fix.

A couple technicians begged to treat him yet he refused. All that mattered was the state of his wife. Luckily, she had only sustained a flesh wound injury. At first they tried to hassle him about climbing in the ambulance with her, but he quickly assured them he was the husband.

Cameron reached out from the stretcher and held his bloodied hand. She had temporarily fainted from shock, but was now alert and aware.

Jude cut his eyes at the angry teen. Cam may've wanted her spared but he planned on making her death look like a suicide once she got to prison.

"I'm gonna blow you to hell, bitch!" she screamed. "Do you fucking hear me?! YOU'RE DEAD! I will never stop coming for you! I will hunt you down and wipe out your entire generation—starting with those fucking half-breed mutts!"

If Cameron had a gun within reach she would've shot Alessia her damn self. She didn't appreciate her coming for her kids. Cam should've popped her ass in the cabin but she decided to have a heart. She'd done the same foolish shit tonight and now she had a damn hole in her shoulder.

"Fuck that young bitch," Jude said, low enough for only them to hear. "I'mma make sure she handled personally. You can bet on that shit."

Alessia was in a total uproar. "You're gonna pay for what you did to my family—to my brothers!" she screamed in the distance.

Cam and Jude paid her useless threats no mind. They knew she was just upset that her plan had been foiled. Now she would be going away for a very long time—maybe even deported. The US government took crimes committed by immigrants seriously.

All of a sudden, Alessia grabbed the service pistol out an officer's holster. She refused to let her arrest be in vain. She was determined to kill Cameron at any and all costs.

As soon as Jude heard the ruckus he looked over and saw Alessia being subdued. The cops were trying to take the weapon away from her.

"Give me the gun!" she screamed. "I HAVE TO KILL THAT BITCH! LET ME GO! I have to f—"

POP!

The gun went off, silencing her immediately. Alessia was so fixed on causing harm to others that she ended up hurting herself in the end. She immediately collapsed in the arms of the police officers.

In the midst of struggling, the gun went off in her hands. There was a dime-sized hole in her chest. She had shot herself directly in the heart.

The policemen gently laid her body on the ground while another touched her pulse. The somber expression he gave afterward told them everything they needed to know.

Alessia was dead.

18

oxie was sitting on the sofa in the living room, staring at the National Geographic channel when Magyc entered the apartment. Prior to him walking in, she was daydreaming about their relationship and if there was any chance it could ever be salvaged. Roxie highly doubted it.

"We gotta talk," he said once he reached her. His expression was neither pleasant nor unpleasant, so she was unable to read him. She couldn't tell what mood he was currently in. Lately, he seemed so up and down.

Roxie climbed off the couch. She had to stand up for what she planned on saying. "You damn right we do."

"You first."

Roxie propped her hands on her hips. "Mothafucka, when was you gon' find time to tell me about your already-made family? 'Cuz this shit right here, I can't even stomach it! I thought we were trying to build together, and you got kids out here? You tearing down what we built! You more fucked up than these bitches out here!"

He didn't expect her to fly off the handle, and it showed in his expression. Magyc was actually about to propose buying a house together. He'd taken some time for himself to think about where he wanted to be. And he quickly came to the realization that he wanted to wake up next to her every morning. Magyc wanted to take their relationship to the next level. However, he was totally unprepared for the bullshit Roxie hit him with. His skeletons were practically tumbling out of the closet.

When he didn't reply fast enough Roxie continued. "A lil' birdie came by the other day and planted a seed in my ear... She even had the son of a bitch with her. And for you to try to keep it such a secret, the lil' mothafucka had the nerve to look just like you."

His mouth tightened. He wasn't all too thrilled to hear that Tara showed up running her mouth. She knew he wanted to keep their child under wraps. Once again she was doing what the fuck she wanted. Acting out of emotions would only land her in a world of trouble with him.

"You just gon' stand there with yo' mothafuckin' mouth open or you gon' say something? And don't feed me no mo' lies 'cuz I stomached enough of yo' bullshit..."

Magyc sighed dejectedly and ran a hand through his dreads. "What could I say? It seems like you got all the mothafuckin' answers."

"What do you think I want you to say? I want you to tell me why you couldn't be real with me! How could you keep some shit like that from me? ME—of all people!" she yelled. "You know every fucking thing about me, Magyc! EVERYTHING! I bared my fucking soul to you and you couldn't even tell me you had a son!"

"When the time was right I was gon' tell you about my situation—"

"*SITUATION*? This a mothafucking child! This is a life! This ain't no mothafucking situation! If the social security office and vital statistics knew, why in the fuck am I the last to get the news?"

"Like I said, when the time was right, you would've fuckin' knew."

"Who the fuck are you, Magyc?" she cried. "Who the fuck are you 'cuz I feel like I don't even fucking know you! Why couldn't you come to me and talk to me? For months you been helping me look after

Rain when all this time you had a son—and one you don't even take care of, for that matter!" she added.

"You don't even know the whole fuckin' story so stop judgin'—"

"I don't have to do that. Your son will when he grows up and realizes what a lousy, piece of shit father you are—"

"You know what? You walkin' a fine line with that one right there. You walkin' a fine line."

"I regret ever putting trust in yo' ass!" she yelled. "And to think, all this time I been laid up with you...fucking, sucking, and catering to your sorry ass! Nigga you ain't shit!"

Magyc waved her off. "Man, you don't even know what the fuck you talkin' 'bout. You throwin' opinions around 'bout some shit that got nothin' to do wit'cho ass!" He never thought she'd make a big deal out of it, but apparently he was wrong. "When you on the outside lookin' in, it's hard to see the complete fucking picture!"

"I can only tell you what it looks like from where I'm standing. And from my view, it looks like you ain't even a man."

"Opinions are like assholes. Everybody got one," he said. "I know what the fuck I'm doin'."

"And what is that? 'Cuz to me it don't look like you doing shit but running from your responsibilities."

"Aye, man, chill the fuck out with dat shit. You really startin' piss me the fuck off wit'cho careless ass talk. You don't wanna push me to my mothafuckin' limit," he warned her. "I'm tellin' you the shit ain't pretty. I can guaran-damn-tee you that."

"Oh, the truth hurt, huh?" she taunted. "I see that bitch start coming out when the truth get too heavy. Nigga, get the fuck outta here. Fuck you and your limit. I mean seriously, what type of fucking man don't take care of his kid? Answer me that shit."

Before Magyc could respond she cut him off.

"No man. No fucking man at all, that's who!"

All of a sudden, Magyc rushed Roxie, slammed her against the wall, and pressed his arm against her throat. He had gotten fed up with her talking shit. She had finally pushed him to his breaking point.

"I ain't a mothafuckin' man? Is that what'chu fuckin' tell me?" Spit sprayed her face as he yelled angrily. "I been takin' care of you and some dead nigga's baby like she mine—'but I ain't no fuckin' man?!"

Roxie couldn't breathe. If he didn't let go soon she would asphyxiate.

WHAM!

Magyc punched a hole in the wall beside her head. It came so fast that she felt the swift wind from it. An inch more and it would've been her pretty face. "You got me fucked up! You'll never meet another nigga that'll do for you what I do!" he hollered. "And if you ever say some reckless shit like that again I'll knock yo' fuckin' head off!"

Roxie slid to the floor coughing and gasping for air. She didn't even recognize him. He was a savage, barbaric animal.

Roxie was finally beginning to see the real Magyc. Briana tried to tell her he was a lot to handle, and she didn't believe it until now. Their honeymoon phase was over and the true colors were shining through. Roxie liked him a whole lot better with the mask on.

"You ain't shit," she said in a hoarse voice. "You hear me, bitch? You ain't shit but a liar, cheater, and fucking deadbeat!"

"Fuck you, stupid ass bitch!"

"FUCK YOU! You ain't shit but a coward!"

"Oh, I'mma coward? *I'MMA FUCKIN' COWARD*?! Find another nigga to play sponsor and step-daddy then. Bitch, I'm out."

Magyc tossed the deuces on his way out the door, and Roxie threw a porcelain jar at the back of his head. Luckily, it smashed against the surface after the door closed behind him.

"Fuck you! YOU AIN'T A FUCKING MAN!" she screamed at the top of her lungs, trying to get another rise out of him. Fortunately, for her, Magyc didn't come back. And she had a strong feeling that he never would.

∽

JUICY WAS AWAKENED the following morning by the sound of her phone vibrating. Rolling over in the queen size bed, she grabbed her iPhone off the nightstand. Surprisingly, it was Rico texting her. The message read:

Good morning baby...

Juicy quickly responded:

It's 7 am. You always up this early? I was still over here dreaming...

Rico replied shortly after:

I try to make all 24 hours count, baby. I go hard for this money, cuz you never know when shit gone get real...

Juicy: *And what do you do, might I ask?*

She waited ten whole minutes but a reply never came, so she texted:

???

Rico: *You like to travel?*

He was purposely avoiding her question.

Juicy: *I haven't done much of it. Honestly the only places I ever been was Ohio and Georgia...*

Rico: *I gotta fly out the country for business this weekend. You should accompany me...*

Juicy: *IDK... I just told you I don't really be traveling...*

Rico: *I know... And it's time you let that basic bitch mentality go...*

Juicy was immediately offended by his last text. "Did this nigga really just call me a basic bitch?" she asked herself. Juicy didn't even bother asking him to explain what he meant by his statement. Instead, she sent a simple message shutting him down:

We're not gonna get along. I can already tell. Just delete my shit.

Juicy attached a peace sign to her text. Rico responded almost immediately:

U kinda crazy huh?

Juicy had no remorse when she replied with:

Fuck you fat ass...

Something told her she wouldn't have liked his cocky, arrogant ass and she was right. Rico never responded, and Juicy hoped like hell that he just forgot about her. She damn sure planned to forget about him.

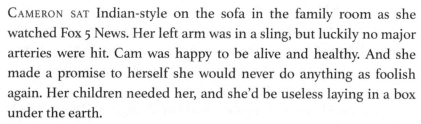

CAMERON SAT Indian-style on the sofa in the family room as she watched Fox 5 News. Her left arm was in a sling, but luckily no major arteries were hit. Cam was happy to be alive and healthy. And she made a promise to herself she would never do anything as foolish again. Her children needed her, and she'd be useless laying in a box under the earth.

Cameron had already seen the footage of Alessia's death, yet she refused to change the channel whenever it aired. At the bottom of the screen was a bold caption that read: **TEEN KILLED BY FATAL SELF-INFLICTED GUNSHOT DURING POLICE STANDOFF.**

Suddenly, Jude walked in the room. "You watchin' this shit again?" There was displeasure in his tone.

Before Cameron could answer, he grabbed the remote and turned the television off.

"No matter how many times you look at that shit the outcome ain't gon' change," he said. Jude took a seat beside Cameron on the sofa. "How you feel?" There was heavy concern behind his words.

"Good..."

"You *look* good." He pinched her bare thigh peaking out of the over-sized t-shirt she wore. He'd left it in her dorm one day back when she was in college, and he hadn't gotten it back since. Now Cameron used it as a pajama shirt.

Jude wanted some pussy but he understood and respected the fact that she had been through a lot.

"Thanks, baby," she smiled.

"I been meanin' to talk to you 'bout some shit... I wanted to tell you the night we renewed our vows but...we ended up gettin' thrown off by bullshit." He didn't feel the need to even mention Alessia's name.

"Wassup?" Cam asked, curiously.

Jude took her hands in his and held them. "I'm givin' the business to Magyc," he confessed. "I want out the game. I see what it's done to you...what it's done to me—to us. I'm finally ready to pass the torch."

Cameron was at a complete loss for words. She searched his eyes for uncertainty but saw none. "You're serious?"

"Do I look like I'm not?"

Cameron faltered with a response. She never wanted to have the responsibility of running the business, but he insisted. Now that he was telling her he wanted out she was practically dumbfounded. "Are you sure you wanna do this?" she asked.

"I've never been more certain 'bout anything in my life. I already started investing money to secure our future. A couple of properties, mutual funds, and businesses will keep us set for a while. I want us to move and start fresh somewhere. I've been thinking about Hawaii."

Cameron giggled. "Hawaii?"

"Hell, it could be Bangladesh for all I care. Long as I'm wit'chu."

Cam looked at him sideways. "So you're really ready to walk away from it all, huh?"

"Took me a while to realize sometimes walking away has nothing to do with weakness...and everything to do with strength. The shit was fun while it lasted but you and the kids are all that matters to me."

Cameron smiled sweetly, touched by his words of compassion. Leaning over, she kissed his forehead, then his cheeks, and then his soft lips. Her arms wrapped around his neck as she gradually climbed in his lap.

Jude grabbed her slim waist, deepening the passionate kiss. Cam slid her tongue in his mouth and gently grinded against him. His rough hands went to her luscious ass and he squeezed hard enough to leave handprints. It had been too damn long since he touched her the way he wanted to. Jude respectfully waited three agonizing months, but tonight he planned on putting another baby up in her ass.

He tugged on the hem of her top, making sure to be extra gentle with her because of her injuries. "Take this shit off," he said, hoarsely.

Cameron obediently did as she was told.

Jude's mouth immediately watered at the sight of her perky

breasts. Like a parched animal, he grabbed them and sucked ravenously.

"Unnh! *Baby!*" Cam's head fell back in delight as his tongue swirled around her nipple.

While he sucked, kissed, and nibbled on one, he softly squeezed on the other. Cam was so wet that he could feel the heat radiating from her crotch. Jude carefully stood and laid her horizontal on the couch. He didn't even feel like going to the bedroom. He wanted her right there and then.

Lowering himself at Cameron's waist, he gently pushed her legs apart and buried his face.

"Jude..." His name left her lips in a sigh. Cameron shivered and trembled as his slippery tongue caressed her clit. When she no longer thought she could stand the foreplay, he climbed in between her legs, and pulled his sweatpants off.

Grabbing his pole, he rubbed the head softly against her pussy. Cameron gasped and moaned in pleasure. Her back arched and her hips moved forward as she tried to catch his thrust.

Jude pushed his pre-cum covered tip against her base. He teased Cam a little by sliding the head in just a little and pulling it out to rub against her button.

Cameron was drenched before he even put it all in. Bucking her hips wildly, she silently begged for all of him—every inch. She needed him and she couldn't stand to wait another second. "Fuck me," Cameron whimpered.

Jude pulled his dick out, slapped it against her pussy a few times, and dove back in. Her fingernails scratched his back as he filled her with slow and steady strokes.

"I wanna make this pussy come everyday, Cam," he whispered. "Can I do that?" Jude tapped her spot repeatedly, making it wetter and wetter. "Can I do that for you?"

"You can do whatever you want to me, baby. I'm yours," she moaned.

Jude pulled out, climbed down, spread her legs, and slid his tongue inside as far as it could go.

"Oh, shit! JUDE!"

Cam subconsciously tugged on his dreads as he licked, sucked, and hummed on her clit. He skillfully used the tip to flick across her bud. Cam's leg's trembled as he held them wide open. When she tried to run, he pulled her ass right back down to his face and devoured her.

"Can I taste this pussy everyday?" he asked in between light kisses to her pussy. "Can I do that for you, baby?"

"Yes, baby, God, yes!" she bellowed.

Jude sucked, French-kissed, and blew on her pussy until she shivered with her first orgasm. He barely gave her time to recuperate before stuffing his massive dick inside.

Cameron was so wet that the couch was soaked beneath them. Jude kissed the side of her neck and the space behind her. His breath tickled her skin making her nipples harden even more. Everything about him, everything he did drove her crazy. "I'm never letting you go. You hear me? I'm never losing you again." He kissed her deeply. "I'll go crazy without this pussy, girl."

Jude's pace sped up, causing her to bust prematurely. He didn't stop immediately; instead he continued to pound Cam until she came a second and third time. He took immense pleasure in satisfying his woman. Just looking at her beautiful sex faces made his dick harder.

"You so damn perfect," he said, gazing in her eyes. "Kiss me."

Cameron snaked her tongue inside his mouth and he sucked it like a piece of candy. His warm cum seeped down the crack of her ass. He had bust well before her second orgasm.

"I love you, Cameron. No matter what we go through I'mma always love you."

19

Roxie frowned as soon as she heard the door to her apartment open. She and Rain were chilling in the living room. Well, technically Rain was knocked out on the loveseat, while she pretended to be interested in television.

Roxie didn't look up or acknowledge him when he walked in the room. She kept her eyes focused on the LED TV like he didn't even exist.

Despite all the shit he talked, Magyc silently took a seat next to Roxie on the sofa. Succumbing to the anxieties of the day, he dropped his head in her lap like a child to his mother.

"I'm sorry," he said, exasperated. "I'm sorry about everything I said. I'm sorry about everything I did. I'm sorry for not keepin' it real wit'chu. I don't wanna fight, bay. I'll be the man you need me to be. Just tell me what I gotta do and I'll do it. I don't wanna lose you, Rox. I ain't ready to walk away from us and what we've built. I promise I'mma change. Just tell me what'chu want. Tell me what'chu need from me. What I gotta do to make you feel secure? I'll do anything in my power to keep you happy 'cuz there ain't no future without you..."

"Magyc, all I need from you is honesty and commitment. That's all I want. Can you do that?"

He buried his face in the soft skin of her stomach. "Yes. I'll do whatever it takes," he said. "You apart of me now. I wouldn't be able to live with myself if I lost you. It'd be like losing part of myself. You make me whole, Rox."

Roxie released a deep breath. He always knew how to break down her walls of defense. What to say to weasel his way back in her heart. Magyc had her ass wrapped around his finger and he knew it.

"Magyc, I love you but I am not gonna compete for you—"

"You don't have to. I'm through with the fuck shit. I'm done gambling on our relationship. Losin' my family ain't worth the risk. I swear, from here on out, I'mma be the man you and Rain need me to be."

"You also need to be the man Marlon needs you to be."

Magyc fell silent. After carefully considering what she was asking he said, "I'mma do what I gotta do."

Grateful towards his willingness to compromise, Roxie leaned down and kissed him. "You have to promise me that from now on it's just me..."

"I promise."

Roxie strongly hoped he kept his word this time.

"Can I ask you a favor?" he said.

Roxie looked skeptical. "You think you in the position to be asking favors?" His ass was still in the doghouse, and there was nothing clever he could say to get him out of it.

"Chill, I ain't 'bout to ask you nothin' crazy, girl," he laughed. "I just wanted to know if you could free up some time tomorrow to look at a couple houses with me."

"Houses? Wow. You really ready to take that leap?"

Magyc slowly stood to his feet and tugged her up as well. "I'm ready to do a whole lot more wit'chu."

Roxie smiled and shook her head. She could only imagine what he was hinting at. "How 'bout you start with the basics."

Magyc kissed her supple lips. "Nah, I'mma start by making you cum."

Roxie broke out laughing when he lifted her up and carried her to the bedroom. As usual, she surrendered to the love of her life. She only hoped her decision wouldn't come back to bite her in the ass.

~

Spent a check on a weekend...
   I might do it all again...
   I just hit a three peat...
   Fucked three hoes I met this week...
   I don't do no old hoes...
   My nigga, that's a no-no...
   She just want the coco...
   I just want dinero...
Travi$ Scott's *"Antidote"* poured through the speakers as Juicy did her thing under the spotlight at Persuasion's. A mass of singles littered the stage and floor. Juicy's individuality, good looks, and acrobatic pole tricks had quickly earned her a spot as one of the customer's favorites. Every time she walked in that bitch she shut shit down.

The other dancers hated whenever she showed up for work. Some of them were even insecure about going up on stage after her. Juicy always left the men in awe, and anyone that followed her engaging performance paled in comparison. None of them would admit it, but Juicy made their asses step their own game up.
   Poppin' pills is all we know...
   In the hills is all we know...
   Don't go through the front door...
   It's lowkey at the night show...
As Juicy did her thing on stage, she noticed Rico swagger casually into the club. That night he was solo-dolo.

Hmph. He must've left the Kardashian at the crib, she thought to herself.

Once again, the strippers colonized around him like he was a star or someone special. *What is it about this nigga that got the hoes going wild?* Rico headed to the bar and his small group of beautiful admirers trailed closely behind. Where ever the money went they submissively followed.

Juicy's turn ended and she quickly scurried to the dressing room before he saw her. As far as she was concerned they were still beefing so she had nothing whatsoever to say to his ass.

In the locker room Dynasty was preparing for her performance. Instead of the shoulder length blunt cut she usually rocked, her hair was styled into a faux hawk. She wore a Gucci slingshot and black leather lace up thigh boots with ten-inch heels. The bitch looked like a gotdamn Avatar with ass shots.

Is it just me, or does this hoe's booty get bigger every time I see her?

Juicy chalked the observation up to her eyes playing tricks on her. Earlier she and Dynasty had split a pill so it could've been easily attributed to that. "D, lemme ask you a question," she said, joining her at the vanity.

"Wassup, Baby Mama?" That was her affectionate pet name for Juicy.

"You ever seen that nigga that be coming in sometimes? Light-skinned, kinda thick with a beard."

"Green eyes?" Dynasty asked, dabbing on perfume.

"Yeah."

"Oh, you talking 'bout Rico. Yeah, I see him from time to time. Why? What about him?"

"What the fuck does he do? Every time the nigga walks in here bitches start flocking to him like he giving away free implants and shit. What gives?"

Dynasty laughed. "Bitch, I couldn't even tell you for real. I never really talked to him before. He seems pretty low-key though. Why? You trying to bone?" she teased.

"Girl, stop. I was just curious, that's all."

"*Mmhmm.* Is he out there now?"

"Yeah."

"Well, why don't you go ask him, hoe? I'm sure he could fill you in a whole lot better than me." With that said, Dynasty walked out of the dressing room, leaving Juicy more curious than she was before.

After freshening up, Juicy remerged in a new outfit. When she scanned the crowd for Rico she didn't see him, and her first thought was that he'd left.

All of a sudden, she felt someone creep up behind her. "All that shit you was talkin' earlier now you checkin' for a nigga."

Juicy turned on her heel and faced him. Right now his eyes were the color of leaves in the springtime, but the shade seemed to change often. His arrogant ass was as fine as he wanted to be. "Boy bye. Wasn't nobody checking for you," she lied.

"Whatever you say," he said, unconvinced. Rico slapped her ass. "Now come dance for this fat nigga."

Juicy stifled a laugh as she followed him to an empty table. As soon as he took a seat, he pulled her down on his lap in a straddling position.

After stuffing a Franklin in her G-string, he pulled her close so he could be heard over the music. "How come ain't no dude snatched you up yet?"

Juicy looked at him incredulously. "How you know I'm single?"

"There's signs," he simply said.

Juicy sighed. She was supposed to be giving him a lap dance, but he seemed more focused on picking her brain. "You want the truth?"

"Shit, that's all I'mma accept," he said. "When you fake you gotta lie all the time. One lie turns into another one just to clean up the first one. The price of keeping it real is way less than the cost of being fake."

"...I haven't found a good man yet," she told him.

"Real niggas still exist. Ya'll just be overlooking 'em. Too busy glorifying suckas," he said. "Now tell me why you *really* single. Enough of the bullshit." Rico saw right through her game. He prided himself on being considerably intuitive, and had no problem whatsoever reading her. He was an educated thug that could've been a psychologist.

Juicy took a deep breath and released it. "I *was* dealing with someone not too long ago... But circumstances prevented us from continuing to see each other."

"*Circumstances*? What'chu mean by that?"

"Bruh, you wouldn't even tell me what you do for a living. Now you expect me to disclose my personal business?" Juicy laughed. "It don't work like that, my nigga."

"Well you tell me how it works then, pretty lady."

"You let me know something, I'll let you know something. And we can go from there," she said.

"Aight then. What'chu wanna know, love?"

"What do you do?"

Rico knew the question was coming before it even left her lips. "I spoil women, upgrade 'em, and show 'em how to get even more on their own."

Juicy looked confused. "What does that mean?"

"What'chu think it means?"

"I'm not sure. It sounds like some pimp shit," she said.

He chuckled. "Nah, I wouldn't call it that. Matter fact, I despise that word."

"So what *exactly* is it you do then?" Juicy asked. She was tired of him dancing around her question.

"I turn females into breadwinners."

"So you *are* a pimp?"

"Every bitch I touch I boss up. I never looked at it as being no pimp. I like to think of myself as a CEO."

Juicy shook her head at him. She just knew his ass was trouble. "That ain't shit but a modern day pimp."

Rico shrugged. "Call it what'chu will."

"Look, I'mma just be upfront. I ain't with all that pimp shit," she said. "Don't be trying to turn me out. You'd better get at one of these other hoes to recruit."

Rico laughed. "Chill. I ain't trying to pimp you, baby. I'm just tryin' to give you long dick and longevity."

"Hold up. Hold up. Let's get one thing clear right now," Juicy told him. "I don't fuck the customers."

20

"Oooh! Shit, Rico! Fuck me!" Juicy cried out.

He had her head buried in pillows and her ass lifted high while he drilled her with 11 solid inches of pipe.

"All that shit you was talkin' in the club now you got this dick up in you." Rico grabbed her waist tight and pounded into her with such force she thought he hated her. "How it feel?" he asked. "How this dick feel?"

"Shit, it's good, baby. Damn, keep hitting it like that. You gon' make me bust!"

Rico snatched his dick out and she squirted all over his belly and thighs. Before him, she didn't even know she could.

Rico greedily cleaned her pussy with his tongue. Every so often she jerked and quivered when she felt it slide inside. She didn't stop him when his tongue slid across her asshole either.

Juicy yelped in delight. Rico was a certified freak.

Lying on his back, he pulled Juicy on top of him in a straddling position. She moved rather sluggishly due to exhaustion, but a firm slap to the rear got her together real quick.

"Get'cho mothafuckin' ass up here, girl. You ain't tired."

In a squatting position, Juicy rode him until his toes curled and face turned beet red. Like two bowling balls, he held each ass cheek to guide her rhythm. Rico wet his thumb and gently massaged her swollen button.

"Damn, bitch. Ride that mothafucka. Make that dick spit."

Juicy climbed off and reversed her position, so he could get a clear view of her backside.

"Gotdamn, girl...I wish you could see what I see," he said. "You know just what'chu doin'. I love that shit."

In a fast-paced motion Juicy rubbed her clit. "*Ooooh,* Rico! I'm 'bout to cum again!"

He grabbed her waist and started bucking wildly from underneath. "That's it. Get that nut off, baby," he coached.

Changing positions once more, she rode him like a horse jockey facing frontward. Rico grabbed her throat rather roughly and pulled her down to tongue kiss.

"This my pussy now," he whispered. "Yo' ass is mine, Diana. You belong to me."

Juicy trembled uncontrollably as waves of ecstasy washed over her. Her body was sweaty and gripped by pleasure. She had never cum so hard in her life. Shortly after, she collapsed on top of his burly chest winded. Beads of perspiration formed on her brow and upper lip.

"I see why they call yo' ass Juicy."

Rico kissed her again.

"And I see why the hoes be flocking to you," she laughed. "You fuck all the dancers with the same stamina and passion? Or am I special?"

"You don't worry about who I fuck. You just make sure you treat this dick right. And I'mma make sure I treat you right."

Juicy laughed and shook her head. "I can't believe I went from despising you to almost liking you."

He chuckled. "Let's not dwell on the past."

She was just about to climb out the bed but Rico pulled her back towards him and held her.

"Where you think you going?"

Juicy felt like she was snuggling with a teddy bear. His body was so warm, and cushy, and soft. "You acting like you don't want me to go," she giggled.

He kissed her neck. "I don't."

"You betta stop playing before your girl comes back and catches us in bed."

"And she gon' climb in and get'chu off next."

"You something else," Juicy laughed. "But I ain't telling you nothing you don't already know." She laid her head and on his chest and played with the soft curly strands. There was a tattooed portrait of Malcolm X on one arm and Mansa Musa—the richest black man to ever live—on the other.

"I ain't gon' flex. It *is* a lot of responsibility that comes with being with a nigga like me. But I gotta feelin' you can handle it."

"How you know I want that responsibility?"

"Only way to know is to find out."

"I might like being independent," she teased.

"Look baby, it's cool to be independent. But it's even better when you gotta real king who can hold you down."

Juicy gave him a skeptical smile. "Oh, so now you wanna be my king?" she asked.

"All I wanna do is be a provider to a woman that's worthy."

A MONTH LATER, Cameron and Jude were on the living room floor coaching their daughter during her first attempts at crawling. He was finally starting to spend less time in the streets and more time with his family. After all, they needed him a lot more than the business did.

As promised, Jude was currently grooming Magyc to take over the empire. He could no longer risk his freedom or the lives of those he loved. Cam and his children meant too much to him.

"Come on, JJ. Come on, boo boo. Crawl to mommy."

"No, come to daddy," Jude said, playfully being competitive.

Justin was opposite of them trying to get her to crawl to him. Journee gurgled and giggled as she looked at her family like they were crazy. When she was first born she looked like Cam's twin, but now she was starting to resemble her father more and more by the day.

Jude's great, great, great grandfather was Aboriginal and it showed in Journee's warm, golden brown undertones. She had a headful of dark blonde hair that made Cam question if she really was Jag's, but a second paternity test quickly confirmed she wasn't. She was 99.6% Jude's.

"Come here, Journee," Cameron sang, stretching her arms out. The Golden Retriever they had just gotten scampered over and licked her face. He was still in the process of being trained, and mistakenly thought Cam was summoning him. "Move, Buddy!" she laughed.

Journee must've found entertainment in Cam being attacked because she started crawling over towards them.

"She's up and at 'em! Look at her go!"

"Hold on, lemme get my phone so I can video record!" she said, leaping to her feet. She quickly dashed upstairs and Buddy eagerly followed suit.

Cameron anxiously ran inside the bedroom and grabbed her phone off the nightstand—

Buddy yelped in pain after she accidentally dropped it on his head. Terrified for his life, he scuttled out of the bedroom and ran downstairs. Cameron froze when she saw a man standing outside their home through her bedroom window. Instinctively, she turned her head away in utter denial. She almost didn't want to believe what she was seeing.

It's not him, she told herself. *He's dead. You're just seeing shit. It's all in your head.*

When Cameron looked back out the window there was no one there. She released a shaky sigh of relief. Once again, the past was coming back to haunt her—but she refused to give in.

Cameron went inside the walk-in closet and fetched one of her shoeboxes on the top shelf. Tucked between a pair of Louboutins was a bottle of prescription pills she kept hidden from Jude. She didn't want him to know how bad the kidnapping had fucked her up mentally. It was something she wanted to keep to herself, because she felt like it would only be a burden to everyone else. She'd already driven her friends and family crazy with illusions of seeing Jag.

Cameron was just about to pop a tablet when Jude walked in.

"Hey, what's takin' you so long?" he asked.

Cameron quickly hid the bottle behind her back in embarrassment. She didn't even hear him come up the stairs. He must've thought something was wrong after Buddy returned to him sniveling and whimpering for attention.

"Nothing. I was on my way back downstairs," she said. Cam couldn't hide the nervousness in her eyes no matter how hard she tried.

Jude slowly walked over to her and reached behind her back. Cameron felt like a child being caught with drugs by their parent.

"What's this, Cam?"

"I—it's nothing. Just a little something to keep me even."

"*Even?*" he repeated. There was a doubtful look etched in his expression.

"It's not that big of a deal, Jude."

Cameron tried to reach for the pills but he moved them out of her reach. "If it ain't such a big deal why didn't you tell me about 'em? Since when do you keep shit from me?"

"I didn't wanna tell you that I was still seeing him."

Jude looked confused. "Who? Jag...?"

Cameron grimaced.

"Cam, don't tell me you still on that shit—"

"I'm not!" she argued. "I—it's...I thought I saw something outside just a minute ago but it was nothing."

Jude walked over to the bedroom window and peered out. All of a sudden, his eyes shot open. "*WHAT THE FUCK!*"

Cameron quickly sprinted to the window to see what was wrong. "What? What is it?!" she asked alarmed.

What Cameron saw made her mouth drop in shock. A horde of

police cars had just swarmed their premises. She'd heard the sirens wailing in the distance, but never thought they'd be coming to her residence.

"Why are they here, Jude? What the fuck is going on?!" Cam asked, panicking.

Jude didn't have time to answer. Instead, he bolted out of the bedroom so fast that he almost tripped in the process. Cameron shoved her phone in her pocket and followed him. Together they descended the stairs.

Jude was on his way to grab the kids when a shotgun shell breached the front door. Cameron screamed when it flew open and a herd of police rushed inside.

They grabbed Jude first, slamming him on the floor hard enough to bust his mouth open. Rushing to his owner's rescue, Buddy ran over and sunk his teeth into the cop's arm.

"Buddy, no!"

"GET DOWN! GET ON THE GROUND!"

Cameron was ruthlessly thrown to the floor and handcuffed.

POP!

Oooowrooo!

Buddy yelped and landed with a soft thud. A single bullet to the head immediately stopped his antics. His furry leg twitched in his final seconds before death.

Jude and Journee screamed at the top of their tiny lungs. They were having a peaceful family moment before the police came and fucked everything up.

"MY FUCKING DOG! YOU SHOT MY MOTHAFUCKIN' DOG! You have no fucking right to do that! You have no fucking right, man!" Jude hollered. The angrier he became the more forceful they became in their restraint.

"JUDE!"

Officers grabbed the screaming children to give to CPS. That's when Cam lost it and tried to go after them. She was grabbed and roughly slammed again by two cops. Her head hit the floor so hard she felt her brain rattle in her skull.

"Don't you fucking touch them! Get your fucking hands off my kids! Don't you—*Ahhhh! AHHHHH!*" she cried out in pain when an officer put pressure on her shoulder. It was the same place Alessia had shot her not too long ago.

"Get the fuck off her! All that shit ain't fuckin' necessary, yo! She didn't do shit! Let her fuckin' go! IT WAS ME! It was all me!" Jude shouted with a bloody mouth. He would die before he let Cameron go down with him.

Unfortunately, the cops were unimpressed by his public display of humility. All they cared about was serving justice. Jude wanted to believe his past demons were catching up with him, but he had a feeling that wasn't the case. There was no doubt in his mind that someone had been talking to the police.

21

"We gotta stop fuckin' around," Magyc said as he pulled his Balmain jeans on.

Baffled, Tara sat up naked in bed and stared at him. "Why?" Her tone was laced with unconfined irritation.

"'Cuz I told my girl I wasn't gon' keep doin' this shit to her."

Tara laughed maniacally—like a female villain in the movies. "Nigga, please. You know you can't stay out this pussy."

"I'm serious," he said, sternly. "This was the last time. So I hope it was as good for you as it was for me."

"Are you serious?"

"Do it look like I'm bullshittin'?"

Tara scoffed and shook her head. "You are so fucking unbelievable it ain't even funny. First, you wanna start playing daddy just 'cuz your girl makes you, now you wanna cut me off to appease this irrelevant ass bitch? This hoe is a non-fucking-factor." It was obvious that Tara was clearly offended. "Do you pray to this bitch before you go to sleep too?"

Magyc didn't appreciate the sarcasm in her tone. He knew his baby mama wasn't going to take the news well, but he needed to do right by his girl—even though it was tougher than he imagined.

If Roxie knew he was still smashing Tara and a few other hoes on the side, she would wipe her hands clean of his ass for good. Magyc knew he was wrong for going back on his word. Roxie deserved faithfulness and a man that wasn't going to lie to her face. Magyc should've been at home with his family, but as always he was dicking around in the streets. Easy pussy was the best pussy for a nigga like him. Like the fast money he'd grown accustomed to making, it had quickly become an addiction.

"Don't get slapped tryin' to be fuckin' cute," Magyc warned her.

Tara twisted her mouth up, unfazed by his threat. "No, I'm dead ass serious 'cuz it seems like she controls you—"

"Don't no fuckin' body control me, aight!" he snapped. Now she was really starting to get to him. Tara had a nasty habit of pushing his buttons whenever she didn't get her way. "Chill out with all that shit."

"It's the damn truth! She commands you like a fucking puppet on strings. You're her little Marionette. Hell, if it weren't for her *making* you be in Marlon's life, you'd want nothing to do with him. *That* is what's most sad," she said. "I don't know who has the bigger pussy! You or her!"

"Bitch, I need you to get'cho mothafuckin' head on straight. 'Cuz right now you makin' me wanna put my mothafuckin' hands on you."

"You ain't 'bout to do shit but run yo' ass home to that bitch," Tara said. "I wonder how welcoming she'd be if I paid her another visit."

"Really? You on that petty ass shit, for real? You wanna talk about me? Bitch, I don't know who was worse. You or Briana."

"Briana's dead. She's incapable of causing the type of destruction I will if you think you gon' keep shitting on me. For three whole years you been giving me the runaround and I'm tired of that shit. I'm done being your doormat and fuck toy. It's either gonna be me or her."

Despite the doggish, neglectful way he treated her, she loved him no matter what he did. Magyc had won her heart at an early age and she'd been smitten ever since. Tara had high hopes of them becoming the family they were always meant to be. Roxie wasn't his baby mama and Rain wasn't his child. She was tired of sharing her man with an illegitimate ass family.

Magyc looked at her like she'd just sprouted a third eye. Surely, she had lost her damn mind making him choose. He wouldn't stand for a bitch he didn't love giving him an ultimatum.

"You know, ya life will be a lot more peaceful when you stop demanding an explanation from who you can't control. Mothafuckas don't owe you shit."

"YOU OWE ME EVERY FUCKING THING!" she screamed. "I'm the mother of your son!"

"That don't mean you fuckin' own me, yo! I'mma be with who the fuck I wanna be with! You don't like it, don't fuck with me then."

"You ain't shit but a lil' ass boy, Magyc. I swear I'm done opening my door for you. You are so fucking pathetic that it disgusts me!"

Magyc looked over at her and felt the same exact sentiment. Right about now just the sight of her repulsed him. He was ashamed of himself for sticking his dick in her to begin with. She wasn't even attractive to him anymore. Tara used to be a voluptuous 160, but she had somehow eaten her way to 230 pounds. There was once a time when she kept her weave tight and nails and feet done. However, over time she'd gotten lazy in the upkeep of her appearance.

"I wish you'd get'cho fat ass on the treadmill and run as fast as yo' mouth do. You so focused on what the fuck I'm doing you done let'cho damn self fall off."

Tara's cheeks flushed in embarrassment. No woman wanted to hear that she was gaining weight.

"You bring yo' ass over to my crib on that bullshit again I'mma fuck you up. Then we'll see how well you run yo' mouth with your jaw wired shut."

Magyc's harsh threat made the hairs on the back of her neck stand.

After pulling on his shoes he headed to the door. "I'm out. I ain't got time for this silly ass bullshit."

Magyc was just about to leave the bedroom when she said something that stopped him in his tracks.

"I'm three months pregnant."

~

JUICY GROANED and stirred softly in Rico's bed. When she looked over he was still sleeping peacefully. Rubbing the crust from her eyes, she reached over and grabbed her phone off the nightstand.

"Damn," she murmured.

Juicy couldn't believe they had slept well into the afternoon, but a late night of fucking could easily do that to two people. Pulling the sheets off her body, she tried her best not to wake Rico.

They had been seeing each other steadily for weeks. He made her temporarily forget about the incident in Cleveland. And though she shouldn't have, because of his profession, Juicy slowly found herself falling for him. Everything about him intrigued her from his looks, to his authoritative swag, to his dexterity. Juicy hung onto every word he said. There was a wisdom about him that came from hanging around older niggas all his life. Rico didn't drink, smoke, or dabble in any recreational drugs. He claimed he always wanted to maintain a sharp focus when it came to hustling.

He was laid back, observant, and knowledgeable. He also invested his time into teaching Juicy to be the same way. Whereas she was always quick to open her mouth and react, he taught her the importance of thinking beforehand.

Juicy grew up in the hood and had been living recklessly all her life, but Rico showed her a completely different world. He even introduced her to his Muslim culture and beliefs. Although he was a young nigga at only 28, she was growing to respect him like a father figure.

Juicy realized that she went for the same type of men because her own dad had never been around. She was always inadvertently searching for that patriarchal figure in her life—and she finally found it in Rico.

He treated her like a queen, never spoke to her disrespectfully, and spoiled her endlessly. His conversations had substance and aggression, and his demeanor shook the tallest of buildings. Niggas

knew better than to step to him incorrectly and all the women loved
and adored him.

The only thing about Rico that bothered Juicy was his vagueness
about his background and past. Anytime she tried to dig he changed
the subject. There was so much mystery and secrecy to him, but his
enigma was what drew her closer.

Rico didn't carry himself like the colorful suit-wearing, cup-
toting, feather hat mothafuckas she always saw on TV. He was an
entirely different caliber.

Rico was exceptional at what he did—a self-proclaimed pro, and
it showed in his luxurious way of living. Every month he dropped
twelve grand to rent out a beautiful mansion tucked off Paces Ferry
Rd. He drove a different foreign car everyday of the week, and he
never wore the same shit twice. Not to mention, his girls were all
financially stable and well-taken care of.

Rico's hustle was on some next level shit. He only dealt with
exotic women who were in the US temporarily for work purposes.
His roster of girls consisted of the baddest broads from Brazil, the
Philippines, Costa Rica, Thailand, Puerto Rico, Columbia, Africa,
Barbados, and the Dominic Republic. After helping them obtain
their work visas—which only lasted 90 days—he flew them out and
showed them how to prosper.

Rico and his girls traveled all over the world, and they did everything from stripping to selling pussy on Backpage and Craigslist. He
also owned a strip club in Old Fourth Ward, where they danced and
catered to rich businessmen on the weekends. Those were the only
days it was open since he moved around so much.

Once the women made all they could, and their 90 days expired,
they went back home to their countries ten times richer. Because they
were immigrants, the lineup changed repeatedly, but the clientele
loved the rotation of new faces. With the exception of a few favorites
that lived with him, Rico was constantly bringing them in and flying
them out. He'd cultivated a loyal customer base through social media.
His IG alone had over a million followers with nothing but advertised

toosh and tits. Rico made seven figures and up doing what he did, and he didn't plan on retiring anytime soon.

Juicy was just about to climb out the bed when Rico pulled her back towards him. "Nah, where you goin'?" he asked in a groggy voice.

"Where the fuck you think I'm going? You know I be having shit to—"

WHAP!

Rico slapped her booty so hard he left a red handprint. "That's what'chu ain't gon' do," he said. "I done told you 'bout talkin' like that. You a lady. Act and speak as such."

He wanted to transform her. Like a work of art.

"Rico, you know I gotta get ready for work soon," she whined.

"You ain't doin' that bullshit no mo'. I'm takin' care of you now," he said, nuzzling his face in the nook of her shoulder.

All of a sudden, two beautiful females walked in the bedroom. Juicy quickly jumped up and covered her breasts with the sheets. She knew he had women who lived with him but she'd never crossed paths with them before. At first she thought they might jump stupid at her but they didn't.

The dark-haired Kardashian chick carried a large tray of food over to the bed. A younger girl followed close behind with fresh-squeezed orange juice.

"Good morning, baby."

"Mornin', daddy."

Juicy watched as both women kissed him on the lips.

"Ya'll made breakfast?" he smiled, eyeing the mouthwatering food.

"Well, actually *I* did most of the cooking," Kardashian beamed. "Amanda was too busy looking through Pregnancy and newborn magazines."

The young girl was infatuated with pregnancy and motherhood in general.

Blueberry pancakes, skillet potatoes, scrambled eggs, hash

browns with mushrooms, and fruit covered the food tray. It all looked so scrumptious.

"Yeah, we thought we'd surprise you with breakfast in bed." The Kardashian looked over at Juicy and smiled. "I wasn't sure if you were hungry but we made you some too."

"Th—thanks," Juicy stuttered, clearly taken off guard.

"Oh, ya'll, my fault. This is Diana. Diana, this is Milena..."

He then pointed to the younger girl who looked no older than eighteen. She was faired-skinned with big eyes and rounded facial features. If Juicy had to guess she'd say she was probably Puerto-Rican.

"And that's Amanda," he said.

Milena said something to Rico in Arabic and they laughed. He was well-versed and bi-lingual, speaking Arabic, Portuguese, and Spanish fluently.

Juicy felt odd and left out since she didn't understand. Were they discussing her?

Milena looked over and smiled flirtatiously at Juicy, like she wanted to get eaten instead. Their overfriendliness made her some-what nervous and bashful.

"This all looks so good, but I—um—I may grab something on the way to the crib—"

"Man, get off that uppity shit and eat breakfast with me. I told you you're done with that bullshit so I don't know what'chu rushin' off for. Ain't no real money in that mothafucka no way. And if it don't make dollars it don't make sense. Shit has to multiply or it doesn't fly." He was forever throwing out catchy colloquialisms. "Besides, I gotta much better gig for you," he said persuasively.

22

"Have you handled it yet?"

Magyc was weaving through traffic on I-75 when he hit Tara up to see if she took care of their issue. He and Roxie were just getting their relationship back on track. The last thing he wanted was a baby fucking up everything they worked so hard for. Magyc made a promise to himself that he and Tara's last time would be their final time. He was done cheating on Roxie, and fucking off. He couldn't lose her.

"Damn, nigga. Just skip the pleasantries, why don't you," she said sarcastically. She was on her lunch break at work when he hit her up with some bullshit. "My day is going swell. Thanks for asking—"

"Cut the shit. Did you do it or not?" Magyc hounded.

"I haven't gotten around to scheduling the appointment."

"Bitch, don't make me have to drag yo' ass to the mothafuckin' clinic by yo' weave. You makin' shit harder than it has to be. You already did what the fuck you wanted to the first time. I don't need no mo' gotdamn kids—especially with a bitch I don't wanna be with! Quit fuckin' stallin' and make the appointment! I'm not gon' play this fuckin' game wit'chu again, Tara."

"What if I don't want to?" she argued. "I may be welcoming the idea of a new baby."

"Bitch, you must've forgot a baby ain't never kept a man at home."

"You can't just force somebody to have an abortion, Magyc."

"Well, you gon' be raisin' two by yo' mothafuckin' self. 'Cuz I don't want shit to do wit'cho ass. And I don't give a fuck about child support 'cuz bitch I got money. So you do what'chu got to 'cuz I'mma do what I got to."

"I DESERVE MORE THAN THIS SHIT, MAGY—"

Magyc hung the phone up on her ass, completely unaware that she was crying. He had no idea of the pain and grief he was causing. She loved him, and desperately wanted him in her child's life, but it was obvious that he didn't feel the same. Still, Tara refused to accept what he was saying. She was in clear denial, and willing to do anything to sabotage his relationship since she couldn't have him to herself.

Maybe I should pay his bitch another visit, Tara thought to herself. Since Magyc wanted to play dirty, she planned on beating him at his own game.

CAMERON WAS RELEASED 48 hours after being arrested. Heavy interrogation about the car theft ring led nowhere and they had no choice but to release her from custody. Unfortunately, Jude was held under further interrogation and suspicion. Cameron's worst fear had come to fruition.

After calling up an Uber, she reached out to Roxie who was temporarily watching the kids. Cameron was grateful that she willingly stepped up to take care of them so that they didn't end up in the system like her. Cam had been bounced around foster homes all throughout childhood, and she didn't want that for her children.

Neither Cameron or Jude had many relatives, but Roxie was definitely the closest thing to a sister. Because of that, Child Protective Services made an exception.

Roxie answered on the third ring. "Thank God you're finally free."

Cameron smiled warmly. "Aww. You missed me?"

"Yeah, but I miss sleeping peacefully even more. Why didn't you tell me Journee cries all damn night? I'm surprised she ain't got a damn hernia yet. And Lord, Justin's so clumsy he could trip over a damn cordless phone. You need to get these chirren checked is what I'm saying."

Cameron laughed, and it really felt good considering all she'd been through. "Don't be blaming my poor babies. You must be over there neglecting them," she teased.

"Hurry up and get these kids before I donate 'em to CPS myself."

Both women laughed at her crude sense of humor. Her children were guiltlessly spoiled and it definitely showed in their behavior. But it wasn't all her and Jude's fault. Magyc and Roxie played a part in it too.

"Alright. I just gotta stop at the store and then I'll be on my way to you."

"Okay—is everything cool with Jude?" Roxie asked. "You haven't mentioned him."

Cameron sighed deeply and ran a hand through her hair. When her eyes scanned the rearview mirror, she noticed the driver lustfully watching her. He quickly looked away so that he didn't seem like a creep, but unfortunately it was too late.

"They still have him, but I'm almost certain they're gonna let him go. They're only going on a tip—just trying to shake us up. They don't have shit concrete to pin on us."

"I hope they do let him go," Roxie said, sadness heavy in her tone.

"You and me both," Cameron agreed. "I'll see you soon though."

"Alright."

Cam disconnected the call and said a silent prayer for her husband to be okay. She wouldn't be able to stand life without him. He had to push through—for her and for the children. He had to come home where he belonged.

Ten minutes later, Cameron arrived at the *Walmart* on Howell

Mill Rd. She had nothing but $50 on her at the time of her arrest, but it was enough to get what she needed.

The Uber driver tried to holler but she politely turned his ass down. Once inside, she grabbed a box of bandages for her shoulder, and a stuffed animal she knew Justin would like. After she purchased her items, Cam ordered another Uber. She was grateful that the driver who picked up her request wasn't the same thirsty nigga who dropped her off.

Cameron was almost out the door when she felt something cold and hard press into the small of her back. She wasn't sure but it felt like a gun. Before, she could turn around a husky voice whispered in her ear.

"Don't turn around. Just keep walkin'."

Cameron immediately got goose bumps after recognizing the familiar voice.

"You're just gonna shoot me? Right here? Right now? In broad daylight?"

"Funny, I remember asking you something similar..."

His voice sounded a little different, but she was certain that it was him. Cameron wished like hell she was hallucinating again. She wanted to believe she was dreaming, but when she felt the cold steel of a loaded gun pressing into her, she knew she wasn't.

"Jag, please—"

"Shut the fuck up, Cameron. I don't wanna hear shit you gotta say. I'm done listenin' to anything that comes out your fuckin' mouth. Keep walkin'. Bitch, try any mothafuckin' thing I'mma blow yo' mothafuckin' head off." Jag mushed her in the back of her head with his gun. "You think this a mothafuckin' game? I ain't playin' wit'cho stupid ass. Now keep walkin' 'fore I empty this fuckin' clip. I don't give a fuck about these people or broad daylight, I'll blow yo' head all over this fuckin' parking lot—and you know I'm dead ass serious."

Tears poured down Cameron's cheeks. She felt like she was trapped in a nightmare. How was it possible that he was even alive? She could vividly recall putting a bullet in his head.

What she didn't know was that he had survived the attempted

murder. Right after she left, a couple hunters stumbled across him and his sister's bodies in the cabin. They'd heard the screaming and gunshots and came to investigate. When they saw the bloodbath inside they immediately called for help. If it weren't for them, Jag would've been rotting in hell. The hunters had saved his life.

Doctors had to remove half his skull to prevent further injuries from brain swelling. It took him two entire weeks just to be able to respond to simple commands by blinking his eyes.

Jag spent months in physical therapy learning how to walk again and talk properly, and his speech could've still used some improving. Cameron had fucked him up physically, emotionally, and mentally. If living the rest of his life with a permanent limp wasn't bad enough, he now had to deal with the loss of his youngest sibling. Jag fell to pieces when he heard the news about his sister. As a matter of fact, he was lying in a hospital bed when he saw the footage.

Jag forced Cameron to walk to the covered parking garage where his car awaited them. Sadly, she wouldn't be riding in the front or back seat. He planned on putting her ass in the trunk for all the damage she'd caused.

"Was it you?" Cameron asked. "The one who narced to the police about the ring?"

Jag's silence said it all. He did tip the police off, but only because he wanted Jude out the way. He knew they would have no choice but to release her under recognizance. Truthfully, he wanted to kill Cam's husband, but he was certain that she would never forgive him.

"Jealousy done turned yo' ass to a snitch, huh? Is that what you do now? You're a real fucking coward, Jag. You could've gotten my babies taken from me! Did that cross your mothafucking mind?"

Jag slammed Cam against his car and pressed the gun to her crown. That instantly shut her up. He was tired of hearing her talk.

This was the first time Cameron saw his face since the day she escaped his clutches. He didn't look the same at all. He was a lot skinnier due to lying in a hospital for months. His once vibrant eyes were now dull and listless. Although he'd changed physically he was still crazier than a mothafucka.

"I should kill you!" he said through clenched teeth. "You tried to kill me...after every fucking thing I did for you. You put a fuckin' gun to my head and pulled the trigger. I LOVED YOU! I loved you with everything in me, Cam! No one's loved you more than me! I killed for you!" Tears filled his deranged eyes.

Cameron expected the gun to go off at any minute. She could only imagine the hatred he felt in his heart for her.

"I should blow your gotdamn head off... But I'm not," he said. "I'm not gonna kill you... You wanna know why?"

Cameron tearfully shook her head. She didn't want to hear shit he had to say. She wanted nothing to do with his psychotic ass.

"Because I love you," he finally said.

Cameron spat in his face after the confession. That was the last thing she wanted to hear.

Jag could've pulverized her, but instead he wiped it off. Her actions only demonstrated that she was truly in need of correction.

"I still fuckin' love you regardless of what you did to me—what you did to Alessia—"

"I didn't do shit to that girl! She did it to her damn self—"

Cam's sentence was cut short after he wrapped a hand around her throat. Jag squeezed so tightly that his nails dug deep into her skin.

"Bitch, if I were you I'd tread very fuckin' carefully," he warned her. "'Cuz if you say the wrong shit, love won't be strong enough to keep me from fuckin' you up!"

Cameron's eyes shot open in fear. She couldn't breathe, she barely could think straight. Her heart was hammering so fast she thought it would beat out of her chest.

"Now this what we gon' do... You gon' get'cho ass in this motha-fuckin' car, and we gon' get our daughter—I'm sorry—*our* children," he corrected himself. "And maybe—just maybe—I won't beat your mothafuckin' ass unconscious when we get home."

Cameron tried to speak, but her esophagus was crushed.

Loosening his grip, Jag allowed her to speak. "What was that?" he asked.

Cam struggled to talk in between ragged breaths. "She's...not your daughter..."

Jag's eyes narrowed but he didn't react immediately. "...I had a feeling..." he said in a low, disappointed tone.

Damn. He's taking it better than I thought he would, Cam told herself.

All of a sudden, Jag punched her dead in the face with a closed fist. He hit her so hard that she fell and smacked her head against the car window, causing it to crack.

A passing young woman witnessed him clock Cameron and stared in amazement. She couldn't believe a man would actually hit a female like that in public.

Jag glared right back at her, his grip on the gun tightening. "Keep fuckin' walkin', bitch, 'fore you be on the ground next to her!"

Terrified by his violent threat, she quickly fled, leaving Cameron to fend for herself. She didn't need those problems.

While Jag wasn't paying attention, Cam quickly grabbed a glass bottle that had missed the trashcan.

Jag looked down at her and she quickly hid it from view. She was still a bit dazed after the vicious blow to her jaw. He had hit her like she was a man who was his height and weight. Jag was unforgiving in his assault, but she didn't get anything she didn't deserve in his opinion.

Cameron struggled to stand. She tasted blood in her mouth, and it felt like he had broken something. She'd never been struck so hard in life. It was as if Jag put all his pent up hatred into that one punch. He wanted her to literally feel his pain and misery.

Pthu!

Cameron spat a glob of dark red blood on the ground. She had no time to recuperate before he snatched her and slammed her against the car. He then wrapped his massive hands around her neck and squeezed the life out of her.

"*You tell me she's not mine?!*" Jag screamed. "After all this fuckin' time! After all the months I spent with her! After all the love I gave her! Bitch, I should gouge your fuckin' eyes out! You stupid bitch! You knew all this time, didn't you?! DIDN'T YOU?!"

Saliva flew onto her face as he yelled at the top of his lungs. Cameron was so afraid that she was shaking. There was blood smeared on her face and fear in her round eyes. No one in life scared her more than Jag. Not Wallace. Not Silk. Not Marcus. Hell, not even the Grim Reaper himself. Jag was the bête noire of her very existence.

He finally calmed down a little and then laughed dementedly. "It's fine. It's cool. A little fucked up," he added. "But it's cool." He leaned in closer, his lips only centimeters from hers. At first she thought he was going to kiss her. "We'll have plenty of time together to make babies."

KSSSHH!

Cameron smashed the bottle over his head and took off running and screaming. "Help! Somebody help me!"

As luck would have it, an off-duty police officer walked out of the store. He still had his uniform on, but even if he didn't, he still would've ran to her rescue. He was strongly devoted to serving and protecting.

"Is everything alright, ma'am? What's going on? What happened to your face?" He quickly reached for his walkie-talkie to call in the disturbance.

"Please! You have to help me!" Cameron screamed. "He's trying to kill me!"

Jag should've fled when he had the chance, but instead his crazy ass walked right up to them. Blood poured down the side of his face. He looked possessed.

"Officer, everything is under control. Me and my wife were just having a small disagreement." He said that shit like he really believed it. "It's nothing serious."

"It looks pretty serious to me," the cop said.

"Officer, I don't know this man!" Cameron lied. "He assaulted me! Tried to kidnap me!" She was desperate to see him arrested and thrown behind bars where he belonged.

The officer looked from Cameron to Jag. He wasn't sure if it was a domestic issue. However, something about Jag seemed sketchy to him. "Sir, I'm gonna need you to put your hands behind your back."

"Are you fuckin' kiddin' me?"

"Sir, I'm not gonna ask you again," he said, reaching for his pistol.

Jag unwillingly did as he was told.

"You have the right to remain silent. Anything you say or do can be held against you."

While Jag was arrested and read his Miranda rights, Cameron discreetly slipped away. She was needed for a statement, but all she cared about was getting far, far away from Jag. She couldn't believe he was actually breathing, living, and walking the earth. She had to figure out her next move, because it just might be the one to save her life. If the law couldn't detain him long, then it'd only be a matter of time before he came after her again—and she wanted to be prepared.

ROXIE SAT with a smug expression as she waited for her unwarranted lunch date to arrive. She couldn't believe she had traded a pedicure for a meeting with her least favorite person—and to make matters worse, the bitch was ten minutes late.

On cue, Tara sauntered inside the restaurant with a devious grin on her pretty, brown face. It was the same diner Magyc had taken Roxie to during their first date.

Roxie was certain that Tara chose that location for a reason. She was obviously trying to get a rise by stirring up feelings. And she chose to take the petty route just to do it.

Tara was luminous that day in a bright yellow blazer, white loose-fitting blouse, and striped pencil skirt. Roxie noticed that she gained a little weight since the last time she saw her.

"Thanks for meeting me," Tara said, plopping into her seat.

"Miss me with the formalities, bitch. What did you call me for? And how did you get my number?"

"The same way I get all Magyc's hoes' numbers. By going through his phone whenever he's sleeping next to me. Oh—I'm sorry. My mistake. You're his *girlfriend*, not his groupie." Tara wasn't even there a whole five minutes before she started throwing shade.

"I gather you're implying that ya'll are still fucking." Roxie folded her arms and mean-mugged Tara. She didn't feel like playing guessing games. She wanted the truth without all the rhetoric, empty talk.

Tara smiled wickedly. "I gather that you're right. But, oh, the plot thickens." She said it like a side chick with pride. She had no shame dealing with a man she knew was in a relationship.

"How so?" Roxie asked, forcing a generic smile.

Tara got straight to the point. Reaching in her Celine bag, she pulled out her pregnancy folder, which contained all the paperwork from her antenatal appointments. With a sly grin, she handed them across the table to Roxie.

"What the fuck is this shit?" she asked with a nasty attitude. Tara didn't answer. As soon as Roxie flipped through the documents her heart lurched. "You called me here to tell me you're pregnant?"

"Magyc wasn't going to so I thought I would do you a favor. If it were me, I damn sure wouldn't wanna be left in the dark."

"And what's you M.O.?" Roxie asked. "You know what? On second thought, don't even tell me. It honestly don't even fucking matter." She stood to her feet, preparing to leave. "You want that cheating, lying ass nigga so bad, you can have him, bitch. Ya'll simple-minded asses deserve each other."

Tara laughed childishly. "Oh, I made you copies, boo. Feel free to take one." She flung a paper at her as she walked past, and Roxie lost it.

WHAP!

"Bitch, don't be throwing shit at me! Have you lost yo' fuckin' mind?!" Roxie swung and hit Tara right in the temple.

The attack caught her off guard, and Tara's first reaction was to kick Roxie. At that point, Roxie was ready to beat the baby out her belly. Before she could drag that ass, management came and quickly broke up their tussle.

"Leave! Right now before we call the cops!" the Supervisor threatened.

"Fuck you! Fuck the cops! And fuck this garbage ass food!" Roxie said on her way out. She was so pissed off that anyone could get it just for looking at her the wrong way.

Roxie hopped in her car and peeled off in anger. As soon as she stopped at the first red light, her phone started ringing. She frowned immediately at the name displayed on her screen. It was Magyc's trifling ass.

Roxie mulled over the decision on whether or not she should send him to voicemail. She would've been more inclined to answer for Jag.

"What, Magyc?" she snapped.

He didn't expect her gruff disposition when she picked up. "Aye, I'm finna text you an address. Meet me there in half an hour, aight."

Roxie wanted to tell him *'go fuck yourself'*, but instead replied, "Okie dokie," and hung up. She couldn't wait to turn up on his ass when she saw him. All the promises he'd made, all of the lies he had told—Roxie had finally had enough of it all.

Her grip tightened on the steering wheel. If she saw him walking down the street at that very moment she would've ran his ass over without a second thought. Tears blurred her vision as she drove.

Why did I ever trust him, she asked herself repeatedly. *Why did I ever believe anything that came out his mouth*?

Suddenly, Roxie's phone buzzed in her lap. It was the address to where he wanted her to meet him. Magyc was in for a rude awakening once she arrived. His problems were only just beginning.

～

"WHAT'S YOUR NAME, SON?"

"...Gambino... Campioni."

The officer turned around and narrowed his eyes at the Sicilian smart ass in his backseat. He highly doubted that was Jag's real name.

Since he'd been placed in the back of his police cruiser, Jag had yet to cooperate.

The first time he was asked for his name, he sarcastically replied, "*Ivan the Terrible.*" Jag didn't fare well when it came to law enforcement, and he'd do anything he could to make their jobs harder.

Avoiding the officer's pensive stare, Jag looked out the window at the passing customers. A few nosey people stared in curiosity, eager to see who'd gotten arrested at a *Walmart* of all places. They assumed he was a thief that had more than likely been caught in the act. Just like that, a contract killer with over 50 bodies under his belt had commonly been mistaken as a petty shoplifter.

Turning around in his seat, the officer typed Gambino Campioni into the computer for a database query. He had no idea that Jag had given him the name of his adopted brother. Ironically, Gambino also dated Cam's best friend, Poca until his tragic murder in 2012. They still never found his killers.

No more than two minutes later, Gambino's information popped up. Everything from his social security number, to his eye color, to where he was born appeared on the screen—right along with the date of death.

"Alright. I'm taking you down to the station and booking you. We'll see how cooperative you are when you're standing in front of a judge."

"Bite me," Jag said.

The police officer shook his head in frustration and started the car. He ran into assholes like Jag everyday, and knew just how to deal with his type.

Jag continued to stare out his window as they hopped on the Interstate. He couldn't believe he let Cameron slip away from his fingers. One minute he had her in his possession and the next she was gone.

An evil grin spread across his face.

It didn't matter. She could run all she wanted, but there was nowhere on the planet to hide. Jag was a professional when it came to finding and killing people—he was virtually inescapable. And it'd only be a matter of time before he sank his claws into her again.

Cameron may've been committed to her bullshit marriage with Jude, but she'd forever be his. With no friends or relatives left in his life he refused to forfeit her too. Jag was determined to be with Cameron—even if he had to force it. Nothing or no one could stand in his way, especially some underpaid prick with a badge.

Jag looked over at the mesh steel cage separating them. There was a small square-shaped opening for them to communicate should he have more questions. Ever so discreetly, Jag slid his cuffed hands under his bottom and over his legs, so they'd be in front of him.

As soon as the officer looked in the rearview, he played it off like he wasn't doing anything. The minute his gaze shifted back to the road, Jag contemplated his next move. He had no intentions whatsoever of sleeping in a jail cell.

"I see guys like you all the time," the cop suddenly said. "You get in these spats with your old lady and then you pretend they're your personal punching bag. You know, for fifteen years I watched my own father beat my mother senselessly—and for stupid reasons. Supper not ready once he gets off work—nonsensical shit like that. She knew there was an underlying problem, but she never realized the magnitude—never even sought help... And then one day, he snapped and killed her." The officer shook his head at the painful memory. "It's despicable...what you did to that girl—whether she was your wife, girlfriend, or some girl you just bumped into—you should never hit a lady. Every time you mistreat a woman, you give up the right to be treated like a man."

Jag's jaw muscle tensed after his last statement. "Have you ever been in love?" he suddenly asked. "And I'm not talking that intense but relatively shallow bullshit I'm talking about *really* in love."

"I've been married for ten years. And even before then I had my fair share of passionate attachments," he admitted. "But what you did to that girl...I could never see myself doing that to any of them."

Jag snorted, and his frown darkened. "Well, if you ever been in love like I been in love you'd know that it can make us do crazy, unjust things sometimes."

Before the officer could respond, Jag reached through the partition and strangled him with the handcuffs. The cruiser swerved uncontrollably as he fought to reach for his service pistol.

Suddenly, it veered off the road and down a grassy slope surrounded by trees. Jag bared his teeth like a sociopathic animal as he strangled the life out of the cop. His crazy really cropped up when he started laughing psychotically.

"You could've died with the dignity of a hero," Jag said. "Now look at your stupid ass!"

The officer soiled himself in this midst of his struggle. The blood vessels in his eyes burst, and his face swelled up like a balloon. Jag didn't stop until he saw the cop's arms drop limply at his sides.

Jag wasted no time un-cuffing himself. Before climbing out the car, he grabbed the cop's gun.

"Hey! Is everything okay?" A concerned civilian asked. He'd stopped to make sure they were safe after witnessing them veer off the road. He was a white guy with strawberry blonde hair, and looked to be in his mid-thirties. He should've been taking precaution when approaching Jag, but all he could think about was lending a helping hand. "Should I call for help?"

Jag pointed the gun at him. "Thanks, but no thanks. I'll take those car keys though."

When he saw the gun, all of the color rushed from the man's pale face. "H—here. Take 'em." With shaky fingers he held out the keys to his Nissan Maxima. He mentally berated himself for not minding his own business like he should've. Everyone else on the interstate kept driving. He wished like hell that he had done the same. "Just please don't kill m—"

POP!

Jag put a bullet right in between his eyes at close range. The innocent man dropped where he stood in a dead patch of brown grass. After carefully wiping his prints off the weapon and handcuffs, Jag strategically planted both on the man. Someone had to take the fall. Just not him.

~

FIFTEEN MINUTES after getting off the phone with Magyc, Roxie arrived at a gated private estate in Buckhead. Magyc's Roadster was the only car present on the property, so she couldn't figure out why he'd called her there.

They had looked at several homes but was undecided on purchasing a property. After everything Roxie learned today, she doubted she'd be taking that step with him anytime soon—or ever for that matter.

When Magyc saw her pull in, he opened the tall double doors that led to the grand entrance. He was stylishly good-looking that day in a long sleeve olive green sweater, fitted black jeans that were torn at the knees, and black Doc Martens boots. A $3000 Raymond Weil watch was the only piece of jewelry he sported. A .45 was tucked in the holster on his waist. Roxie would never understand how a convicted felon like him got his CCW rights restored.

After parking next to his sports car, she quickly climbed out with set intentions. A severe scolding was on the tip of her tongue, but Magyc cut her off before she could even speak.

"How you likin' the exterior, bay?" he asked, happily. "Driveway's big enough to park 15 cars. Five for you and ten for me." Magyc laughed at his own corny joke, and Roxie remained stone-faced. She didn't see a damn thing funny.

Her ill-natured attitude completely flew over his head. He was so excited for her to see the house that he didn't even notice. Taking her by the hand, Magyc eagerly led her inside the luxurious seven-bedroom home.

There were marble floors throughout, unrivaled amenities, a resort-style swimming pool, a fully equipped gym, theater, and tennis court out back.

"I wanted you to see it before I closed the deal on it," he said.

"This is the one. I know it, Roxie. I can feel it. More than enough space for us, more than enough room for Rain to grow."

Roxie frowned at the mention of her daughter. After today, he would never spend another second with her.

"And you haven't even seen the best part yet," he told her.

Roxie begrudgingly allowed him to pull her inside the living room. All of the curtains were drawn and the lights were off, making the room unnecessarily too dark. She wasn't at all amazed by what she saw when they walked in. Spelled with lit candles on the floor were the words *Will You Marry Me*?

When Roxie turned around to look at Magyc he was holding a tiny velvet box with the lid lifted. Nestled inside the white slit cushion was an 18K diamond solitaire.

"I love you so much. And I don't wanna waste anymore time, Rox. I'm ready to be a family. I wanna wake up next to you everyday for the rest of my life." he said. "Let's make it official, baby... What do you say?"

Roxie scoffed. "*What do I say*?" she repeated. "I say it'll make a damn good congratulatory gift for Tara."

Magyc's smile quickly faded. He didn't expect her reaction at all— no man would after such a carefully thought out proposal. He assumed everything was fine between them, but clearly he was wrong. Roxie had come from leftfield bringing up Tara.

Magyc knew that he was going to ask Roxie to marry him, and he was confident that she'd accept. That was why he wanted to break things off with Tara, before he fully committed. It was the main reason behind him pressuring her to get the abortion. He thought he'd be able to sweep his dirt under the rug, however Tara had her own hidden agenda. One that didn't involve being deserted so he could have his happy ending with Roxie.

"What'chu mean by that?" he asked.

"Oh, stop it, Magyc! For God's sake, just stop it! Stop acting fault- less! You know good and damn well that bitch was pregnant! How could you do that to me?" Tears rose to her eyes as she yelled at him. Her voice cracked with overwhelming sadness and emotion. She felt like she didn't even know Magyc. "You saw how torn up I was about the miscarriage! And you went and got some other bitch pregnant?! WHAT IS WRONG WITH YOU! What the fuck is wrong with you?! You knew..." Her voice trailed off after she broke down crying hysterically.

Magyc tried to console her, but she slapped the shit out of him.

"DON'T TOUCH ME! Don't ever fucking touch me!" she screamed. "I trusted you! I let you in my home, in my heart—and in my daughter's life! How could you do that to me?! I would *never* do something so foul to you—or anyone I claim to love! And then you have the nuts to propose?! Fuck you and that mothafucking ring! You could choke on that shit for all I care!"

She tried to leave but Magyc stopped her. "Roxie, wait. Why you doing this, baby? You gon' let that irrelevant ass bitch tear us apart like this? She ain't even pregnant," he lied. At that point, he was willing to say anything to keep Roxie in his life. He was desperate. When it all came down to it, he really didn't want to lose her. No amount of pussy in the world was worth that. He only wished he'd realized it sooner.

"I saw the fucking paperwork, Magyc! Stop lying!"

"Man, that bitch could've had that shit doctored up!"

"And pigs fly, mothafucka!" she said, sarcastically. "Save that shit, Magyc. I don't wanna hear it."

"It's the truth!" he argued. "She just mad a nigga ain't droppin' attention on her ass. Don't let her come in between us—"

"Your cheating ass ways came in between us! And to make it worse, you're still standing in my face, lying about getting her pregnant! Are you gon' tell me you were never fucking her still, too?"

"I swear on my niece I haven't!"

"I'm not fucking impressed that you're swearing on her! Your niece is dead," she said, cynically. "What more can happen to her?"

Magyc grimaced but didn't comment on her statement. He didn't want to say anything else stupid. "Roxie, you gotta believe me. I ain't been fuckin' with that girl, man—"

"Stop fucking lying!"

"I'm not fuckin' lyin'!"

Suddenly, Roxie snatched the pistol out his holster, and unflinchingly pointed it at him. "For once, I want the gotdamn truth!" she yelled. Tears and mascara ran down her chocolate cheeks. "Is this what I have to do?! *Huh*? Point a fucking gun at your head to get the mothafucking facts?!"

Magyc tried his best to remain undisturbed, but secretly he was shaking inside. No man wanted to stare down the barrel of a gun held by a brokenhearted woman. It was every cheater's worst nightmare.

"Man, put that shit down, Rox," he said, calmly. "I ain't playin' wit'chu. You put a fuckin' gun in my face you better be ready to pull the trigger." His tone and icy stare was menacing, yet he held his composure well considering the circumstances.

"Maybe, I am," she said. "Maybe I am ready to pull the trigger for all the pain and heartache you've caused."

Oh, this bitch really done lost it, he thought. Magyc never doubted she was a little crazy, but he didn't think she was capable of murder. Then again, everyone had their breaking point. Evidently, Roxie had finally reached hers.

Just when he thought she might actually shoot him, Roxie slowly lowered the gun. "I want you out of my house and out of my life. You and me... we're done."

A LOADED TAURUS rested in Cameron's lap as she sat in an upholstered rocking chair. She didn't feel safe leaving her children unattended so she stayed in their nursery with them while they slept.

Although one of Jude's bodyguards was staying in the guest suite, she would rather be safe than sorry. It was a little after 3 a.m., but she refused to succumb to slumber. After the fiasco with Jag earlier that day she couldn't. Now that she knew he was alive, she had a hard time letting her guards down—and that included sleeping.

Cam tried her best to keep her eyes open, but every so often, she found herself dozing off. She would catch herself in mid-slumber, and jerk awake, looking around the room petrified.

This ain't no way to fucking live, she told herself.

Cameron used to sleep with a pistol back when enemies were gunning for Jude. That was why he'd hired Jag to look after her in the first place. Never in a million years would she have thought she'd need protection from him one day.

Cameron looked over at her children's crib, where they slept peacefully. She would die before she let them end up with Jag again. Cam's grip on her gun tightened. She was like those kids in *A Nightmare on Elm Street*—desperately fighting sleep to avoid something bad happening.

Unfortunately, with all of her efforts, Cameron was still visited by the sandman. She slept four hours before she felt a hand gently touch her shoulder.

"Cam...?"

Her eyes shot open and she quickly reached for the gun—

"No, no, don't shoot! It's me, bay."

Cameron relaxed when she saw her husband standing over her. She didn't even realize she had dozed off. Jumping to her feet, she hugged him like she hadn't seen him in years, even though it'd only been a few days.

"I missed you, baby," he said, holding her tight. "I'm sorry I was away—I should've b—"

"He came back!" Cameron cried. "He's alive!"

"Who?" Jude asked, confused.

"Jag!"

Jude took a step back from Cam and lightly grabbed her shoulders. "Cam, we been over this shit so many times. That mothafucka's dead—"

"No, he's not! He's alive!" she argued. "He attacked me in the parking lot at the grocery store! I had to get the police involved! I swear, on everything I love, I'm not lying! I'm not going crazy! It wasn't a hallucination or a figment of my imagination. He was real, Jude! He's alive!"

"*Ssh, ssh.* Okay. Calm down," Jude said in a soothing voice. Truth be told, he didn't believe her, but he wouldn't tell her that for fear that it would hurt her. He simply figured the stress of them being arrested had gotten to her. "If he shows up here, I plan on handling that mothafucka personally. You can bet on that."

Cameron looked up at Jude with tearful eyes. He wasn't as alarmed as he should've been, and she knew that he doubted her. Cam felt like the boy who'd cried wolf. If Jude fully knew what Jag's crazy ass was capable of, he wouldn't have been so lax. If nothing else, she at least hoped he'd watch his back. Jag was out for blood... and he wouldn't stop until he got what he wanted.

~

I KNOW when that hotline bling...
    That can only mean one thing...
    Ever since I left the city you...
    Got a reputation for yourself now...
    Everybody knows and I feel left out...
    Girl you got me down, you got me stressed out...
    'Cuz ever since I left the city, you...
    Started wearing less and goin' out more...
    Glasses of champagne out on the dance floor...
    Hangin' with some girls I've never seen before...

Drake's latest club banger had the crowd in *Blue Flame* amped that night. Roxie couldn't believe she was back in her old stomping grounds. But since she had broken up with Magyc, she had to take care of herself and her family. And stripping was all that she knew. Like Cameron, Roxie had started dancing at the tender age of eighteen. She'd tried the 9 to 5, but it just wasn't for her. Dancing afforded her the fast cash she'd grown accustomed to.

Roxie had fucked with nothing but niggas who had money. What did she look like going to work at a fast food restaurant full-time? She needed big bucks to pay her heaping amount of bills and expensive rent. Minimum wage just wouldn't cut it. Magyc would've flipped if he knew she was right back where he strictly forbade her from returning.

You and me we just don't get along...

You make me feel like I did you wrong...

Going places where you don't belong...

Ever since I left the city, you...

You got exactly what you asked for...

Running out of pages in your passport...

Hanging with some girls I've never seen before...

Roxie looked delectable in a hot pink one-piece with gold body chains and a collage of cupcakes on the front.

A passing guy stopped to admire what he saw. "Damn, I bet'chu taste as good as you look," he said. "You so bad you should spank yo' own ass twice a week."

Roxie gave a courtesy laugh. He wasn't too attractive, and his breath smelled like he'd been nibbling on pieces of shit. But all money was good money in her line of work.

"I'm about to go up soon. After I come down and freshen up, I'mma come find you and dance for you," she said.

He looked her up and down one last time like he wanted to devour her whole. "Yeah, you do that," he said before walking off.

All of a sudden, Spider ran up to Roxie and hugged her. "Oh my God! I thought that was you who walked in earlier! Bitch, it's been forever! You finally outta retirement?"

Spider was the Anastasia Sokolova of Blue Flame, hence her name. That girl could do every flexible, acrobatic trick there was on the pole. She was definitely one of the top money makers in the place, and a good friend of Roxie's.

They used to keep in touch all the time before Magyc came and tied her down. She'd lost contact with a lot of her old associates. Being in a relationship could easily do that to a person.

"Yeah, I had to. A bitch ain't got that net no mo' if you know what I mean," Roxie laughed.

"Oh, I already know how that shit be. Well, it's good to see you. You look good," she smiled.

Roxie doubted she'd be saying that if it wasn't so dim inside and she could see her scars. She had put a little makeup and concealer on them, but MAC could only do so much.

"Thanks, boo."

"Oh, damn. Did you hear about ole' girl, Lark?"

"Nah, why?" She and Roxie were cool too once upon a time.

"Girl, somebody killed that bitch. Ain't that crazy? Dumped her fucking body in a river not too far from here. That shit was all over the news and shit. I can't believe you didn't hear about it."

Unfortunately, Roxie had been dealing with her own dilemmas. She had no idea Lark had been killed until now. "*Wow*. That *is* fucking crazy. She was hella cool too. Who would wanna hurt her?" Roxie didn't know Jude was the one responsible for ordering her murder. In his mission to break Jag, he ruthlessly took her life without penance.

"I know right. But anyway, off that depressing ass shit. It's good to see you again. Get'cho money, boo, I know I am."

Spider playfully slapped Roxie's ass and sashayed off. That's when she noticed that another dancer had taken her turn.

"*Unh-unh*. Hell no. What the fuck is this bitch on?"

Roxie didn't want to cause a scene so instead she went to the DJ booth. "Sam! I was next!" she whined.

"Baby girl, I ain't even know you was here. My fault. I'mma add you to the rotation now. You go up after Temptation."

"How many girls before Temptation?"

"Lemme see." He looked down at a hastily scribbled list of names and counted. "Fourteen."

Roxie sucked her teeth. "You may as well have said tomorrow," she sassed. She was anxious for her turn to get rained on. All of her old regulars were there that night and she knew they were going to show her love now that she'd returned.

"*Aww*. Don't be like that, Rox. You gotta start making your presence known."

"You can't skip me to the front of the list?" she asked. She gave him a syrupy smile for added effect but he didn't budge.

"Man, you ain't finna have these hoes at my neck," he said. "I don't need dem problems. That's why we gotta system."

Roxie started to walk off but he asked for a hug to make sure there was no bad blood between them. She granted him one since they went back to high school days.

The DJ didn't miss his opportunity to grab on her booty. He'd had a crush on her since the 10th grade.

"Nah. None of that while we beefing," she teased, moving his hand away.

When Roxie descended the stairs to the booth, she noticed a group of young, swagged out Asians walk in.

Roxie did an automatic double take when she realized they were the same guys from the mall. And the one who was checking her out the hardest seemed to be the ring leader.

I guess I better work the floor since I ain't hitting that stage no time soon.

Roxie went and found her stank breath admirer over by the bar. After collecting $50 off him, she went back to the dressing room to freshen up. She also checked her phone to make sure there were no missed calls or texts from Rain's babysitter. Thankfully, there was none but she had a shitload of messages and voicemails from Magyc.

He'd taken the breakup hard, and he didn't want to accept that it was over. When he moved out he tried to purposely leave shit behind so he could have a reason to come back. But Roxie dropped his belongings off on his brother's doorstep and left it at that. She didn't want to play those dreaded back and forth games. He tried giving her money as well but she refused it every time. She wanted nothing to do with Magyc. He'd left her no choice but to treat his ass like trash. *Put out and stay out.* Magyc made his bed and now he had to lay in it.

Fifteen minutes later, Roxie reemerged from the dressing room. The place looked even busier than it did before she disappeared. She was just about to work the room when she felt someone gently grab her arm from behind.

"Hey, excuse me?"

When Roxie turned around she saw the cutest pair of light brown slanted eyes.

"Hey, it's my boy's birthday. You wanna come give him a lap dance? This is his first time in a strip club." The young Asian guy was upbeat and excited. She could tell he was just happy to be surrounded by ass and titties.

"Sure. Where ya'll at?"

He tucked two Franklins in her garter belt, and pointed to a VIP section in the back that was already crowded with strippers, fellas, bottles, and dollar bills.

Oh, I'm bullshitting. That's where I should've been at all along, Roxie told herself. They were definitely the liveliest in the club.

"He's right there," he said, pointing to the only guy seated.

Well, I'll be damned...

Roxie couldn't believe the birthday boy was the same one giving her googly eyes at the mall. She could tell he was shy and she found it rather adorable. He looked cute and comfy in an oversized ribbed sweatshirt, light blue jeans, and $800 Bogetta Veneta suede boots. His style was very modern day Kanye West-esque. He wasn't that tall. Perhaps 5'11 at the most, and slim but fit in frame.

He is just too damn fine for words.

All of his friends were turned up, popping bottles, and throwing cash. But he was low-key, chilling like he was at a cookout or something.

"Hey there," Roxie said, joining him. "I hear it's your birthday. Why you over here looking like you ain't having fun?"

He politely sat up and greeted her. "I am... I—uh—just don't do this often. To be quite honest, I don't really know *how* to act," he chuckled.

"From what *I* was told, you don't do this *at all.*"

His cheeks flushed and he automatically cut his eyes at his friend who slinked off unashamedly. He was mad at his boy for putting him out there like that.

"No...I haven't..." he finally admitted.

"Well, that's cool. I'll be sure to make your first experience your best experience."

His left eye twitched just slightly after she said that. He knew what she was implying, but there was so much more to the meaning —at least, for him it was.

"How old did you turn?"

"Twenty-five."

"Well, happy birthday."

"Thank you."

"I'm Roxie, by the way." She extended her hand.

"Seokwon. But everyone calls me Kwon."

Roxie was surprised by how incredibly soft and supple his hands were. They felt like baby's skin, like he soaked them everyday in natural oils. It didn't make any sense how smooth they were.

"Nice to meet you, Kwon."

"The pleasure is all mine, Ms. Roxie."

Majid Jordan and Drake's newest track had just ended and Bryson Tiller's *"Don't"* started playing. Roxie stood and prepared to dance for him. She thought about getting fully naked—like she usually did— but decided against it. He already seemed a little nervous. She didn't want to give him too much too soon.

I'm back and I'm better...

I want you bad as ever...

Don't let me just let up...

I want to give you better...

Baby it's whatever...

Somebody gotta step up...

Girl I'm that somebody...

So I'm next up...

Be damned if I let him catch up...

It's easy to see that you're fed up...

I am on a whole 'nother level...

Girl he only fucked you over 'cuz you let him...

Fuck em girl I guess he didn't know any better...

Girl that man didn't show any effort...

Roxie moved and winded her hips to the rhythm of the mellow song. Kwon had a donkey and double D-breasts in his face, but he hadn't taken his eyes off hers once. She was so damn pretty to him. She looked like a black porcelain doll.

Roxie straddled him and proceeded to grind in his lap. Kwon's soft hands glided along her thighs and it gave her chills. She was supposed to be dancing for him but he was stimulating her instead. Her nipples hardened from his gentle touch.

Despite her initial thoughts, Roxie went to remove her top—but he quickly stopped her. Pulling her towards him, he whispered in her ear. "When can I see you in regular clothes?"

He smelled of peppermint and Clive Christian cologne. Everything about him was perfect.

"I usually don't like to give my numbers to customers," she smiled, knowing damn well she wanted to give him play. "I try to avoid getting caught up."

He looked disappointed by what she said, yet her next set of words was a pleasant surprise.

"But I *might* make an exception..."

Kwon's dark eyes lingered on her full lips. He almost looked like he wanted to kiss her. "You know what the best thing about today is?" he asked.

"What's that, birthday boy?" A flirtatious grin played in the corner of her mouth. He was devilishly handsome, and he knew it.

"Seeing you again..."

Roxie tried not to blush. She actually thought he had forgotten. Kwon smiled at her and it warmed her heart. *I might've just ended a relationship, but that doesn't mean a girl can't have new friends.*

"DAMN. SHE STILL AIN'T FUCKIN' answerin'," Magyc said, hanging up. He was at the bar calling Roxie like crazy, but it was obvious that she didn't want to talk. He would've blown his top if he knew she was in a strip club caking with a new prospect.

Magyc wasn't ready for it to end. He didn't want to walk away from what they had. *Man, we been through too much shit for her to just throw us away like this. She knows how fucking much I love her. I may not be perfect but I tried to give my all to her. And I loved her baby girl like she was my own. How could she just abandon what he had?*

Magyc failed to consider the amount of chances she'd given him. Roxie had put up with more than enough shit before finally calling it quits. Instead of taking responsibility, he blamed her for giving up on them.

Magyc downed his shot of whiskey straight, no chaser. He'd been tossing them back nonstop since Roxie gave his ass the boot. He could've stayed where ever he wanted, but instead he temporarily crashed on Jude's sofa. Cameron didn't mind, and he was glad because he really didn't feel like being alone.

"Damn, I fucked up. I really fucked up," he said, shaking his head. In the game of love, Magyc had lost.

All of a sudden, his phone started ringing. He anxiously reached for it, believing it was Roxie. However, he sighed deeply when he saw Tara's name on his screen instead. Magyc quickly answered the call, and didn't give her a second to speak.

"You know what, bitch? You pathetic! Trying to get a mothafuckin' sympathy card. That's *my* mothafuckin' bitch. I run that shit. You runnin' yo mouth to my bitch. You ain't do shit but show me how to deal wit'cho ignorant ass. I'mma pay my mothafuckin' child support and leave yo' simple ass alone. Now the next time you bring yo' ass to where I lay my mothafuckin' head at, bitch, I'mma split yo' mothafuckin' wig."

Tara just laughed off his insults. "Your selfish ass made me everything I am," she said. It was true. Magyc was indeed responsible for turning her into a coldhearted, cynical bitch. But since he didn't want to account for his actions he simply hung up.

Click.

Magyc didn't want to hear shit her silly ass had to say. He was already upset that she went blabbering in the first fucking place. In reality, it was his own damn fault. If he'd been faithful from the jump, then none of this would be happening.

When the bartender saw the distressed look on his face, she slid him a complimentary shot. She knew he was having girl problems, and was patiently waiting on the chance to take him off Roxie's hands.

Magyc saluted her and tossed it back. He was sick with it. Roxie had him depressed and all fucked up in the head. He'd give every dollar in his bank account for another chance to make things right.

Magyc was so busy drowning in his sorrows that he didn't notice his ex-girlfriend Briana's brothers walking up on him. The beef they had with Magyc far exceeded his beef with Jag. You would've thought he was the one who pulled the trigger the night she was killed. In all actuality, they just wanted someone to blame since they couldn't get close to her real killer.

"You sure that's him?"

"Nah, that ain't him."

"Mothafucka, that *is* that hoe ass nigga."

Magyc was solo that night and unprepared for any drama or bullshit. Lost in thought, he was oblivious to the twittering commentary behind him. The only thing on his mind was his girl.

"Aye? You Magyc?" a deep voice asked.

Magyc didn't even bother turning around. "Who the fuck wants to know?"

"What was all that shit you was poppin' at B's funeral?"

Before he could answer, the eldest brother busted a bottle over Magyc's head.

JUICY, Rico, and five of his girls were all seated at a table in the 4-star *Tomo Japanese Restaurant*. Juicy couldn't believe she'd allowed him to drag her into his chaotic world. He had a complex occupation that involved dealing with dozens of girls regularly. But the only ones Juicy saw were the quintet that lived with him. Life was hectic for a man in his profession and that's what he needed Juicy for.

She was sort of like an assistant manager to him, alleviating some of the responsibility that quickly became overbearing for one man. Rico loved his bitches, and enjoyed doing what he did, but sometimes he needed a break—and someone to pick up the slack.

Much like she did with Cameron, Juicy ran his Instagram page, dealt with bookings, handled the girls' photo-shoots, and scheduled all flights. Despite the work load, she found unexpected pleasure in being something similar to a Madame.

Since Juicy had been in the adult entertainment business for so long and put so many girls on she agreed to his position. She didn't have to shake her ass anymore, she didn't have to fuck anybody, and Rico paid her better than any club ever could. He wanted her to move in too, but she wasn't ready for all that. She still was trying to get used to his anarchic lifestyle. However, Juicy did understand and respect the game. She'd even grown close to the five women who lived with him. And although they all resided under the same roof and loved the same man, they were as different as night and day.

Milena was Middle-Eastern, the oldest, and the diva of the bunch. Sometimes she and Juicy fucked around and had threesomes with Rico. She loved expensive, high-end shit, and buying and wearing designer clothes. Rico always bitched her out about spending more than she earned.

Delany was a beautiful Congolese woman who was 8-months pregnant. One of her regulars knocked her up, before getting life in prison. She refused to get an abortion or put it up for adoption. This would be her first baby, and the girls were all excited to help her raise it.

Delany had no relatives or friends in America other than those she lived with. She had a tough life growing up in the Dominic Republic of Congo, but she didn't let it define her. She was mad cool and the most level-headed of all the girls. One night, when Juicy pulled her to the side, she asked Delany if she liked being with Rico. She surprised Juicy when she stressed that Rico had "saved" her.

Amanda was the youngest at only 18 and *obsessed* with pregnancy. She had a 60" inch LED TV in her bedroom, where all day she would watch reruns of TLC's *A Baby's Story*. She collected pregnancy paraphernalia and magazines as a hobby, and could talk about babies for hours.

At 13, she got knocked up after consensual sex with her stepfather, thus starting her infatuation with babies. Although she miscarried at 4 weeks, she had been smitten with motherhood ever since. Niggas had to strap up twice with her, because she was always trying to get pregnant.

Needless to say, Delany was her favorite person in the world, and she followed her like a trained dog—but that didn't stop her from stealing her ultrasound pictures behind her back.

Amanda was extremely book smart and witty, and yet there was just something off about her. When Juicy asked Rico about it, he blamed it on her having a hard life and being abused by her parents.

Amanda was legally an adult but she had the mentality of a 15-year old. She was oftentimes childish, bratty, and desperate for attention. Despite her juvenile behavior, she made a killing when she danced at clubs, and could work the fuck out of any pole. She even had her own set of regulars. Evidently, some niggas liked sticking their dick in crazy.

Rico found and took Amanda in when she was only 17 and living on the streets. Like Delaney, she claimed that Rico had saved her.

Flo was the drama queen and cry baby of the bunch, hence her nickname. She was a cute German-born bi-racial girl with light brown eyes, a face full of freckles and golden brown hair. She was also a know-it-all and the most annoying.

Flo left home at the age of 18, and moved to America to pursue an education and modeling career. Her parents couldn't afford to pay for her school and send her off. She had to choose one or the other, so she chose the latter. She figured she could get a job and pay her own tuition.

Flo found a gig working as a waitress at a mom and pop diner, but it paid little next to nothing. One afternoon, Milena and Rico walked in, put something in her ear, and the rest was history. When she quit her job to work with him, she started making so much money that she temporarily forgot about going to school. Now, two years later, she was finally chasing that dream again after Rico had to get in her ass. Just because they were making a ton of money didn't mean he wanted them to fail at everything else in life. He was proud of her. And although she was extra at times, she was definitely the brightest of all his girls.

Kina was a 23-year old Laotian girl who didn't speak much English. One of Rico's connects who worked at the jail hit him up when she was arrested for not having proper papers to be in the US. She was a struggling immigrant like Delaney and Flo.

Instead of booking Kina and possibly having her deported, the officer called Rico, who paid him handsomely in exchange for her. He helped her get proper documentation, and showed her a better life. She didn't talk much, she barely smiled, and she hardly ever interacted with the girls. For the most part, she pretty much stayed to herself. Kina, like the others, felt indebted to Rico. He had all rescued them in some fashion or another, and they were extremely loyal to him in return.

"I have another appointment coming up in a couple weeks," Delaney said while they waited on the food. She was due in four short weeks, but looked ready to pop any day now.

"OMG! Please can I go with you again?! I wanna see her itty bitty hands and feet! I need to be there! After all, you said I was godmother when she's born! Please can I go, Dee? Please, please, please!" Amanda said, excitedly.

"Aye man, calm yo' fuckin' ass down!" Rico snapped.

Amanda immediately ceased her theatrics.

Every time Juicy was with them she felt like she was watching a hood version of *All in the Family*. She'd never seen him actually put his hands on them before, and Amanda was really the only one he had to snap off on sometimes. As crazy and unusual as they all were, it was just like anybody else's dysfunctional family—only there were tons of cash, strippers, and prostitution involved.

"Actin' like you need Ritalin all the damn time and shit. Chill sometimes, ma. It don't be dat serious. Just be pretty and benign. All that extra shit ain't necessary. Feel me?"

Just then the food arrived piping hot and fresh. It was only seven of them but they ordered enough for twenty people.

"Oh, I have great news!" Flo announced. "I just got my acceptance letter from Spelman in the mail yesterday." She pulled the neatly folded paper out her purse and proudly brandished it.

"That's wonderful, babe."

"Congratulations," everyone said in unison. Milena was the only one who didn't speak up since she had her head buried in her phone, texting.

"I'm not surprised at all. Baby, you created your own reality. I knew you could do it," he noted with approval. "In life, you do ABC to achieve XYZ, and it finally paid off. I'm proud of you, baby girl. And anything you need along the way to help you succeed you know I got'chu."

Juicy was in awe by the way he treated them. Rico didn't talk or deal with them like they were prostitutes. He treated them like family, and he treated them equally.

"Thanks, Rico...and I just wanna say if it wasn't for you I—" Flo's voice choked up and the waterworks came. As usual, she was about to go into crybaby mode. "I'm sorry. I can't even talk. I need a minute," she said, rushing off to the bathroom.

"OMG, what a drama queen," Amanda said.

"Aye, M? Who you over there typing an essay for?" Rico asked Milena.

She hadn't stopped texting since they sat at the table and it was finally getting to him. Whenever they weren't working, he wanted their attention to be solely focused on him.

"It's nobody—"

"Let me see it then."

"I said it's nobody. Damn. I'm putting it away. Don't make a Federal Case out of it."

Rico's face was schooled to utter calm, despite the way he felt inside. He overlooked her condescending tone instead of slapping the shit out of her. "I don't like repeating myself. When I repeat myself I get frustrated. And when I get frustrated I get violent. And, well, we all know what happens when I get violent…"

Juicy looked round-eyed at him. She had never seen that side of him before.

Every once in a while, Rico had to get a little aggressive. If he didn't keep his bitches in check, his house and business would crumble.

Thankfully, Milena handed it over before he had to get physical. Rico frowned when he saw the tasteless texts and nude photos sent between her and some nigga she met in the mall.

"For all these pics you sent, this better be yo' mothafuckin' highest paying customer."

"I met him at Perimeter. I'm working on getting him to come check me out at the club."

"He don't need to now. He done already seen all ya assets," Rico said. "I told you 'bout sellin' yourself short. There's a difference between being valued by a man and being liked by a man. Know the distinction." Rico spoke the truth, always. And he defied any of them to go against him.

Milena pouted. She really liked buddy, but it was clear that Rico wouldn't let her date him if he wasn't making more than six figured annually. None of the girls were allowed to fuck with a nigga who couldn't do more for him than he could. At least Delaney's baby daddy was a filthy rich kingpin before getting life. That was the only reason he didn't flip when she got pregnant.

"You always correcting me or telling me what to do," Milena sulked.

"You damn right I am. 'Cuz I would never tell you nothin' wrong. And that's the end of the subject. We not finna argue 'bout it."

All of a sudden, Juicy's phone buzzed with a notification. She pulled it out and read over the email. A group of high profile lawyers were throwing a bachelor's party for their colleague and needed dancers.

"We just gotta request for another booking," she said.

"They send the specifications?" Rico asked. The businessmen paid top dollar for the girls but they were the pickiest too.

"Yeah, they did."

"What are they?"

"They w—" Juicy's voice trailed off after she read something she didn't like.

"What?"

"I don't even wanna read this ignorant shit," she complained.

"Why? What it say, bay?"

"No brown-skinned girls. Only white, Spanish or fair-skinned dancers—"

"Aye, they like what they like," Rico told her. "You can't fault 'em. As long as the money good, that's all that matters. Don't let your emotions get in the way of your logic. Don't catch feelings, baby girl, catch Franklins."

Across the table, Amanda was rubbing the life out of Delaney's round stomach.

"Yo, stop touchin' D and let her fuckin' eat, damn," Rico snapped. Dealing with the 18-year old was like having a child and he didn't have any at all—that he knew of.

"I don't mind," Delaney smiled. "The baby really likes when Mandy rubs my belly. She's always kicking and trying to say hi."

"That's 'cuz she knows her God mommy loves her very much," Amanda said in a baby's voice.

"Well, the shit's gettin' on my damn nerves," he said, brusquely.

Amanda stopped rubbing Delaney's stomach just so she wouldn't have to hear his mouth.

Rico looked over at Juicy. "See what the fuck I gotta deal with?"

⁓

THE NEXT DAY, Cameron, Roxie, and Juicy all met at T.I.'s new restaurant, *Scales 925* for food, drinks, and hookah. Cam was still paranoid about Jag coming after her so she had a shooter not too far from where they sat and a gun in her bag. If Jag tried to run up on some crazy shit she had no problem making his ass taste steel. She also made sure to call and check up on Jude and the kids periodically.

Cameron knew she couldn't quarantine herself and family to keep safe. All she could do was watch her back and try to be as alert as she possibly could. She didn't tell her girls about the incident in *Walmart*—at least, not yet anyway. She was afraid that they wouldn't believe her like Jude. They were just as tired of hearing about Jag as her husband was.

"So I broke up with Magyc," Roxie finally blurted out. "And I'm not talking a temporary split to clear my mind. I mean, it's actually *finito*."

"Damn... I'm sorry."

"Sorry to hear that," Cameron and Juicy said in unison.

"No, don't be sorry for me. Be sorry for him. He's the one who lost out on something real. He wanted to run all over the city sticking his dick in these gold-digging bitches and now he can do it with no restrictions. Let them have his lying ass. I'm done. The final straw was finding out that Tara was pregnant—"

"WHAT?!" Cam yelled.

A few nearby people turned their heads to look at her after the random outburst.

"He got that bitch pregnant again? Oh, hell no. He ain't shit," Cameron said.

"My point exactly," Roxie agreed. "Anyhow, on a better note, I met someone new recently."

"Damn, bitch. You don't waste no time, huh?" Juicy teased.

"Why should I? I already wasted enough time on Magyc's ass."

"Amen to that," Cam said, holding up her drink.

She was all too familiar with relationship drama and turmoil. Luckily, she and Jude overcame all of the trials and tribulations that almost ended their marriage. Cam wanted to believe the same could happen with Roxie and Magyc, but he just couldn't seem to do right by her. He didn't even have enough respect not to cheat while she was laid up in a hospital. Cameron was just as disappointed in him as Roxie was.

"Anyway, it ain't too serious. We haven't even gone on a date yet. We've just been texting and Face Timing every once in a while."

"Will we get a chance to see or meet him one day?" Cameron asked.

Roxie grinned like a sneaky, secretive child. "If he's worthwhile...*maybe*," she said.

"Since we're throwing out confessions I may as well drop mine," Juicy piped up. "Ya'll remember Rico, right?"

When Cameron and Roxie verified that they did, she went on to explain his unique occupation and the responsibilities he had enlisted her to do.

"Girl, I would be very careful if I were you. And I would definitely be cautious about dealing with him," Cam warned her. "You don't wanna get caught up in that shit. I'm telling you, you really don't."

Juicy waved her off. "It ain't like that. He has a really good thing going. Very intricate and organized."

Cameron looked at Juicy like she had just lost her mind. "Bitch, are you retarded? You sound just as gullible and brainwashed as them silly hoes he pimping."

Juicy shrugged. "Call it what you want but we getting skrilla."

"Okay then, J. You got it all mapped out it sounds like." Cameron wouldn't dare argue with her about the choices she made. Juicy was a grown ass woman free to think and act for herself.

Since they'd both dropped their bombs, Cam thought about mentioning Jag, but decided against it. All of a sudden, her phone started ringing. Cameron's heart started beating fast when she saw that it was Jude. She automatically assumed something was wrong.

"Hey, baby. Is everything okay?" she answered, trying her best not to sound alarmed.

"No...it's not..." he said, drearily. "Is Roxie with you?"

Cameron looked over at her. "Yeah, she's sitting right next to me. Why?"

"What is it?" Roxie asked, concern in her tone.

Jude released a deep sigh. "It's Magyc..."

CAMERON, Roxie, and Juicy rushed to Emory Hospital and found Jude and Michael in the waiting room. They each had somber and weary expressions, and Cam immediately thought the worst.

"Is he okay?"

"What happened?" Roxie asked, frantically. An hour ago she couldn't stand his ass. But just because they weren't together didn't mean she stopped caring.

"All I know is some nigga's jumped him in the bar. Nobody's came out and told us anything about his condition yet."

Roxie started crying and Michael quickly pulled her close and held her. Magyc wasn't shit half the time, but her life would never be the same if he perished. "It's aight. Bruh gon' pull through, lil' mama. He's a fighter."

The doctor finally walked into the waiting room, wearing a blank expression. Everyone hung on pins and needles as they waited on the final verdict.

"How is he doing, Doc? Please tell us something good," Roxie pleaded.

Michael rubbed her back to soothe her. She was absolutely livid.

"Aside from a few stitches and some internal bleeding, he's expected to make a full recovery."

Everyone breathed a sigh of relief.

"Can we see him?" Roxie asked, impatiently.

"Certainly."

Though she asked for all of them, they insisted she go in solo first to spend a little 1-on-1 time with him. When she walked in, he was lying in bed looking like Miguel Cotto after a boxing match. The amount of L's Magyc had recently taken was ridiculous.

Roxie couldn't help but cover her mouth when she saw him. Briana's brothers had really worked him over.

Magyc smiled and tried to sit up when he saw her. "Damn, is it *that* bad?" he asked.

"Who did this?" Roxie asked.

"It don't matter."

"Was it your ex's brothers?"

"It don't matter," he repeated. "All that matters is *you* here. I'd get my ass kicked again if that means being able to see you."

"This doesn't change anything, Magyc."

He held his bruised hand out for her. "Then let me change your mind," he said. "It's not too late to start over, baby."

Roxie stared at his outstretched hand. She wanted to take it— Lord, knows she did, but she just wasn't ready to open that door again. Magyc had hurt her so many times in the past. He'd left her in turmoil and heartache after finding out Tara was pregnant. Did she really want to put her trust and faith in him again? She had already given him more than enough chances.

"Magyc, I... I can't..."

"Roxie—"

"I just came to make sure you weren't dead," she said coolly. "I have to get back home to Rain." Fighting back tears, she turned and walked out of the hospital room.

Magyc was left with a pained expression and broken heart as he sat alone. "Roxie, come back," he called out. Tears filled his eyes. "Roxie!" He couldn't believe it was really over between them, and had a hard time accepting it. He didn't want to live a life without her. "ROXIE!"

～

WITH ALL OF the drama and crazy shit going on lately, Jude decided to step up his game, and do something special for his wife. That weekend they flew on a private Boeing jet to Kihei, Hawaii.

"You sure the kids will be okay?" she asked Jude for the hundredth time. Jag had her overly suspicious of everything.

"Yes, babe. They're good. Stop worrying. Everything is copacetic."

Cameron relaxed and sipped her wine. She really did need a quick getaway and she was overjoyed when her husband proposed one. After a taxing twelve-hour flight, they touched down on a private landing strip several miles east of their final destination.

"I know you're tired but we're almost here," Jude said with a wide smile.

Cameron couldn't wait to see where '*here*' was. Lugging their suit-cases, they climbed in a town car awaiting their arrival and embarked on their short trip.

Fifteen minutes later, they arrived in front of a beautiful 6-bedroom house situated right along the waters. "Jude, oh my God," Cam said once she saw it. Her eyes were round with enthusiasm. The ocean-front house was more astounding than their vacation home in Thailand.

"It's already paid for and everything," he said. "All we gotta do is move in."

"When?"

"Next month we'll pack up and ship everything over. I wanted to sooner but all that shit with Magyc popped off. So what'chu you say, bay? You with it?"

Cameron reached over in her seat and hugged and kissed him excitedly. "I'm with you where ever you decide to go, baby."

After climbing out the town car, Jude gave her the keys to the crib, and let her explore while he settled in. Besides the panoramic ocean view the home featured an enormous chef's kitchen, an elevator, two guest suites, a game room, a wine cellar, and a beautiful modern pool out back surrounded by palm trees.

The living room opened up to the spacious patio looking out at the water. A grill, bar, and all the amenities needed to entertain guests were out back.

The house had the best location and offered magnificent views. Every day they'd be able to see the sunrise and sunset.

"How you like it?" Jude asked. He walked up behind her and wrapped his muscled arms around her waist.

"Jude it's beautiful—perfect."

"*You're* perfect," he said, kissing her neck.

Cameron turned around and stared into his soft brown eyes. "Thank you," she said. "For never giving up on us."

He kissed her forehead. "That'll never happen."

Cam pecked and playfully bit his chin. She loved every single thing about him. "So what're we gon' do once Justin's ready for school?"

"I was actually thinking about getting the kids homeschooled," he said. "I don't want 'em fed that insubstantial bullshit they teach in public schools. I want them learnin' some *real life* shit."

"Justin's bad ass ain't gon' do good with that," she laughed. "He'd terrorize that poor instructor. At least, he'd be balanced in a classroom."

"We'll figure it out when the time comes," he said.

"What am I gonna do out here as far as work? You think a boutique could thrive?"

"It can. Maybe one day you could get into writing too. We definitely got that type of setting. I can see you typing right out there on the patio. You could write a book about your crazy ass life," he laughed.

Cameron laughed too. "Boy, nobody would wanna read that shit."

"I doubt it," he said. "You see that master bedroom yet though? Shit's huge."

"Not yet. I've only toured the first level."

Jude took Cameron by the hand and together they entered the elevator. She loved how the doors were glass so she could still look at the beautiful interior. She wasn't even going to ask him how much he spent on the house. Everything Jude did was grand and impressive. He had her and the kids spoiled. Jude worked hard to give her the life she came to love.

Cameron broke out laughing as soon as they walked in the bedroom. "You are too damn much. You know that shit?"

Their bedroom was expansive with ten-foot ceilings and a skylight. The north wall was completely covered in glass. The only furniture in the room was a California king canopy bed and slipcov-

ered chair in the corner. Directly in the center of the room was a tall, brass dance pole.

"Shit, you gotta keep in shape, right? What better way than entertainin' yo' nigga?"

"I can't believe you," she said, shaking her head. "Place is barely furnished and yet you made time to buy a damn stripper pole."

Gently pulling her by the hand, he led her towards the bed. "C'mon. Let me know you ain't rusty."

"Whatever, Jude. You know I ain't get rusty," she giggled.

"Show me. Prove it."

"Boy, you know I don't even do that no more," she whined. Cam was already tired and he wanted to see her backflip on a pole.

"Just one dance," he said.

Cameron shook her head and laughed. "Oh my God. Fine, okay. You know I spoil you, right?" she teased.

Jude chuckled, and took a seat on the edge of the bed before pulling out his phone.

"You gon' record me too?" she laughed.

"Nah, I'm finna put some music on."

Cameron kicked off her shoes and pulled her top over her head. Jude moved his dreads out his face to get a better view. A few seconds later, Tory Lanez "*Say It*" started playing.

Grabbing the pole, Cam slowly strutted around it in a sensual manner. She looked sexy in nothing but a black Victoria's Secret pushup bra and a pair of skintight DSquared jeans. Since she was barefoot, she moved with the precision, rhythm and grace of a ballerina.

Jude lustfully watched her climb the pole halfway before doing an elegant spin. When she came down, he curled his index finger and beckoned her to come closer. He could no longer contain himself. He wanted her just as badly as he did the day they met.

Jude didn't take his eyes off Cam's as he unbuttoned and roughly snatched her jeans down. Her panties came off next and he leaned in and licked her pussy—

She gasped and tried to push his head away. "Baby, I should probably shower first. That was a long ass flight—"

"Girl, I don't give a fuck about that."

Jude picked her up and placed her down on the pillow top mattress. After pulling off his Givenchy tee, he climbed down at her waist, and buried his face. Cam bit her lip and ran her fingers through his dreads.

As he pleasured her, she found herself wondering how she could've ever been without him. Once he made her cum from sucking on her clit, he slid in between her thighs.

Cameron fumbled with unbuttoning his jeans. He barely pulled them down all the way before slipping inside her. Cam's back arched as he penetrated her with 10-inches.

Jude sensually glided his tongue along her neck. He kissed and nibbled her chin a little, and sucked her bottom lip like a piece of fruit. "I love you, Cameron," he whispered.

"I love you too, baby."

"I'm not losing you again," he said.

"You never will..."

ScHOOLBOY Q'S "GROOVELINE PART 2" poured through the speakers of Rico's strip club. Since ScHoolboy was his favorite rapper he kept that nigga in rotation. It was packed on a Saturday night and some of the baddest women Juicy ever saw strutted through the place in nothing but bikinis and heels. With all of the beautiful women Rico dealt with she wondered how he could happily share a bed with just her every night—save for Milena, occasionally.

Check the forecast, it's wavy Q...

I should make the news...

My fortune said that I'll be pimpin' you and your pussy juice...

Super sweet, sell a trick a treat...

Hope your lips in shape, 'cuz you worked yo feet...

As you stroll them streets...

Juicy walked through the club, making sure everything seemed in order. She was a part-time manager and house mom so there was always something to do. Rico was in the back office handling business, counting money, and probably getting his dick sucked by one of the bitches. He was quite the corporate thug.

Juicy was on her way to join him when a group of drunk niggas stopped her. "Damn, you one of the baddest mufuckas in here. What'chu gettin' into for the night? You should roll with us."

"I have plans," Juicy said smugly.

"When you gettin' up on stage then?"

"I'm sorry. I don't dance on stage."

"Shit, you *need* to be dancin' on this dick," another said.

She tried to walk around them but they blocked her path.

"Damn, why you runnin' off, baby? We make you nervous or some shit?"

One boldly grabbed her ass.

"Look, I told ya'll I don't strip. Okay? It's over twenty other girls here ya'll can harass. I'm just the manager."

"Oh, I got somethin' you can manage, bitch."

"Is there a problem?" Rico asked, walking up.

The dancer that left out his office with him disappeared inside the bathroom to wash the bitter taste of cum out her mouth.

"It wasn't one. Might be now though," the apparent leader said. They didn't know Rico was the owner, or that he had a gun tucked in his waist with a silencer screwed on.

"Fuck is you? Her man?" the other asked.

"Nah...her soon-to-be-husband," Rico corrected him.

A smile pulled at Juicy's lips after hearing that. She didn't know if it was game or if he was being serious, but it sounded nice either way.

"Oh, is *that* right? Well, nigga she soon-to-be gang-fucked. How you feel 'bout that?" When he bravely stepped in Rico's face all hell broke loose!

The bartenders grabbed shotguns from underneath the counter, Kina pulled a razor out her mouth, and Milena busted a bottle on the table to use as a weapon. They were ready to kill for their beloved procurer. They'd do anything for Rico; twist a blunt, take the rap, and murder in cold blood. They were as loyal as they came. Once, Juicy had asked if he had any male friends and he replied there was no need. She finally understood why.

After realizing they were outnumbered, the assholes backed down and left the club in one peace. Rico could've easily had them killed where they stood, but he didn't want the blood in his carpet, or the task of cleaning up the mess.

Now that all was in order, everyone carried on with their tasks. Juicy was just about to find something to do to keep herself busy when she saw a familiar face walk in.

"...What the *hell* is he doing here?"

Juicy wanted to disintegrate when she saw him. She wanted to vanish, or just flat out disappear. Nothing could've prepared her for seeing Wayne some five-hundred miles from home. What the fuck was he doing in Atlanta? Why in the hell was he at Rico's club? And more importantly, how did he find her?

Juicy's night had gone from bad to worse.

Wayne spotted her over by the bar and walked over. She thought about running, but her legs wouldn't budge. *Is he coming to start trouble*, she wondered. They hadn't spoken since the accident, and Juicy wasn't quite sure where they stood. Maybe he blamed her wholeheartedly for his son's death. If she were him, she would have.

"Hello, Diana," he said once he reached her.

"Wayne, I—hi...How...why are you here? I mean—"

"Can we go somewhere alone and talk in private?" he asked, nervously.

"Is it *safe* to be alone with you?"

Wayne gave her a sympathetic, softhearted look. "Is that what you think I came here for? I would *never* hurt you, Diana. Ever," he stressed. "I do wish you had the same consideration for me though."

"Wayne—"

"You just left. Disappeared. I needed you, D. I..." His voice trailed off and there was a faraway look in his eyes. "I went through hell and high water to find you," he said.

"Why?"

"...Tabitha divorced me," he finally said. "She took the kids, my money, and my home... I'm fucked up." Wayne looked like he was on the verge of tears.

It took everything in her to avoid saying '*not my problem.*'

"I'm lost. So, what? You expect me to move you into my place and take you now that Tabitha don't want you? Look, Wayne, I'm really sorry about everything that's happened but—"

"You can't turn me away now, Diana," he said. "I tried to do the best I could by you in spite of my situation."

"It wasn't a situation. You were married—"

"Don't shut me out just 'cuz I'm a lil' down on my luck now. I lost my son behind this, for Christ's sakes. Show some humility for a man that once spent over $20,000 on you a month—"

"It's not about the money, Wayne! It's not about any of that shit." Juicy paused. She hesitated with telling the truth. She already had a boo, and Rico damn sure didn't share. *Just tell him there's someone's in your life*, her conscience scolded. Technically, there were some *people* in her life, but he didn't need to know all the details.

Before Juicy could be honest, Rico walked up and joined them. He'd been intercepting all night like a football player.

"Who's your friend, Diana?" His gaze deliberately slid over her head to look at Wayne. There was a phony smile plastered on his face, and only she picked up on the irritation in his tone.

Wayne held his hand out. "Wayne Baxter. I'm Diana's boyfriend."

Boyfriend?

Both Juicy and Rico's eyes got big after hearing that. She was unsure as to when they'd started using labels. Wayne was surreptitiously laying it on thick. However, forcing himself on Juicy wouldn't win her heart over.

"Tariq Haddad," he said, shaking his hand. "I'm the owner."

Juicy was surprised that he didn't act belligerent.

"Nice to meet you. Quite an establishment you got here."

"*Shukran.* 'Preciate it, brother. I just like to introduce myself whenever I see a new face," Rico told him. "Aye, Scarlett, give my man a round," he said to the bartender. Rico patted Wayne on the back in a friendly manner. "What'chu drinkin, brother?"

"Scotch'll be great," he said.

As Wayne reached for his drink, Rico noticed the branded Greek-letter scar on his upper forearm. "What fraternity did you pledge?" he asked, curiously.

"Alpha Phi Alpha," he said, proudly. "Cornell University. Graduated '96."

"Up in Ithaca, right?"

"Yes sir." Wayne sipped the liquor.

"Interesting. I'm from New York myself. Attended Syracuse University but dropped out my sophomore year."

Juicy stood idly by listening to two men she had feelings for chatter. She felt some kind of way that Rico was opening up more to Wayne than he ever did with her. She didn't even know his last name until tonight.

"Hey, well, you know college isn't for everyone," Wayne said. "But things definitely look like they turned out good for you anyway."

"'Preciate it. Aye, you pretty cool, man. I get a good vibe from you. Why don't you let me show you around really quick? I just had the VIP suite remodeled. First lap dance will be on me."

Wayne looked at Juicy to see if it was okay with her and she just shrugged.

"You don't mind if I steal him for a second do you, Ms. Diana?"

Rico was trying to be funny, but the only thing he was doing was pushing her buttons. "Do you," she said, dryly.

The last thing she heard was him mention sports to Wayne before they walked off.

"Bitch, who was that?" Milena said, walking up. "He was finer than a mothafucka."

Juicy waved him off. "Nobody. Just an old friend."

While they talked shit, Rico led Wayne through the club and towards the rear exit doors. Since he'd never been there before, Wayne naively believed he was being taken to VIP. He was sadly mistaken.

As soon as Wayne saw the exit sign he realized something was wrong. Before he could ask why he was there, Rico shoved him roughly through the doors. Wayne staggered a bit but didn't fall. You would've thought he was a loser being tossed out for making trouble while drunk. Unfortunately, Rico's beef had nothing to do with Wayne's alcohol consumption, and everything to do with Juicy. He didn't want Wayne coming and fucking up what he had going with Juicy.

"Aye, man, what the fuck is yo' prob—"

WHAP!

Rico punched his ass so hard in the jaw that his back molar flew out. Wayne dropped to the ground instantly. Flo and Kina walked outside in their stripping attire. They'd saw Rico leave with Wayne and knew some shit was about to pop off.

"You stupid mothafucka. You got a lot of balls showin' yo' mothafuckin' face around here!"

Wayne tried to stand but was dazed after the brutal blow. "I should've known your ass was full of shit," he said with a swollen cheek. Wayne knew right away that Rico was fucking Juicy. He just wished he would've peeped game sooner. Wayne spit a mouthful of blood onto the asphalt. "We fuckin' around with emotions, huh? I ain't know a piece of pussy would make a mothafucka wanna throw blows. I never had to fight for a woman."

Amused by the older man's bravado, Rico chuckled.

"You right," he said. "I *don't* fight for women."

PHT!

Neither woman blinked or flinched when Rico put a bullet in his skull.

Wayne's body hit the ground with a hard thud, his eyes still open.

"Get this stupid mothafucka off my property. I'm tired of lookin' at his pussy ass." Rico tucked the gun back in his waistline and turned to leave. He didn't have to remind his girls to make sure it didn't trace back to him. They were no strangers when it came to covering up his tracks.

Rico stepped inside the club and left the two women to it. He found Juicy over by the bar still talking to Milena—who *secretly* was keeping her distracted.

"Where's Wayne?" Juicy asked, looking over his shoulder.

"He left. And you ain't gotta worry about that mothafucka no more."

"So, what is it that you do?" Roxie asked Kwon over dinner at *Canoe*. This was their first official date and she wanted to pick his brain a little.

"I—uh—I'mma DJ," he said, rather quickly.

Because he faltered, Roxie automatically assumed that he was lying. "*A DJ*?" she repeated with sarcasm. "Didn't expect that. What's your DJ name?"

"...DJ Kwon," he said.

Roxie gave him a skeptical look. "I don't know why I anticipated something cleverer and more creative."

"Was that shade?" he laughed.

She laughed with him. "I'm sorry. I don't mean anything by it. It's just...it took me for surprise. I'll just say that," she said. "So where do you DJ?"

"You wouldn't know it. It's a club in Seoul."

"Is that where you're from."

"Yes. Born and raised."

"Do you live there still?"

"Yes."

"So you're just visiting Atlanta?"

"Yes, for business..." he said. "But a certain someone recently made me extend my stay."

"Aren't you sweet," Roxie gushed.

"What about you?" he asked. "I'm not that interesting. Tell me something about you. Where are you from?"

"Georgia-bred, baby." She smiled and it made his heart flutter.

"Do you travel a lot?" Kwon asked.

"From time to time."

"Have you ever been to Asia?"

"No. I wouldn't mind visiting one day though."

"Maybe we can arrange that."

Roxie blushed. For some reason, she found herself picturing what their babies would look like. "So," she began. "You ever dated a black girl before?"

Kwon's cheeks flushed and it was the cutest thing she'd ever seen. "Does it matter?" he asked.

"Well..."

"I don't think it matters," he said.

"It doesn't...but I'm kinda curious."

"Next question," he chuckled.

"Okay, then. Do you have kids?" she asked.

"No. But I would love to have some though—after marriage and everything, of course," he added.

"Are you good with kids?"

"Yeah, I love them. I have a bunch of nieces and nephews. I'm very good with all of them."

Kwon pulled out his phone and showed her pictures of him and his loved ones.

"Are these your sisters?"

"Yes. I have five in total. No brothers."

"They're really pretty. Wow, you've got a big family, Kwon."

Roxie looked over all the photos. His life was fascinating to her. She could tell he came from wealth. "Who's that?" Roxie asked. She pointed to a suited older man who wore a no-nonsense expression. He hadn't smiled in a single picture.

"My father."

"And what does he do? He looks presidential."

"He's...a businessman," was all Kwon said.

"*Unh-huh.* So how would they act if you introduced me?"

Kwon hesitated. "Honestly, I'm not quite sure."

"*Aha!* So you've never dated a black girl!"

A few people turned in their seats and scowled at Roxie.

"I didn't say that," he said. "It's just that most of my family have never left Korea. Therefore, they've seen and had limited interaction with different cultures."

"So what you're saying is they might be racist."

Kwon laughed. "That's definitely *not* what I'm implying," he said. "Let's just put it this way, whoever I decide to love they will respect, no matter what. They have no choice but to."

Roxie wanted to know what he meant by that. But instead of further probing, she chose to drop the subject—for now. "So," she began. "I just have one more question and then I'm done with my lil' interrogation. I promise."

"It's no intrusion at all. Please...ask away," he insisted.

"What are you looking for? Casual dating or a relationship?" She wanted to know his intentions so that they were on the same page.

"I'm hoping casual dating eventually leads to a relationship. But I wanna pace it accordingly."

"Well...I just got out of somethin' myself.... So we can be friends but I'm not looking for anything more."

Kwon's lips curled into a grin. "Yeah...you say that now..."

MAGYC WAS HEATED when one of his boys texted him a pic of Roxie and Kwon leaving the restaurant. He worked for valet as a front to steal cars for the ring. Needless to say, he recognized his friend's girl immediately. The message was even accompanied by a text that read:

This yo girl or nah???????????????

It was embarrassing, disrespectful, and infuriating to Magyc. "This bitch left my ass in the hospital to fuck with Jackie Chan? Yo, is she fuckin' serious right now?"

Roxie hadn't seen the fucked up side of him yet. If there was one thing he wouldn't tolerate, it was her dealing with another man. He didn't give a damn if they were together or not.

Once you fuck with me, you stuck with me.

That was Magyc's unwavering view and he stood firmly behind it.

This bitch is in for a rude awakening, he told himself. *And that motha-fucka she running around the city with finna end up dead in an alley some-where. I put money on that shit.*

~

"WHAT'S WRONG WIT'CHO ASS? You been distant as fuck these last two weeks. Wassup?" Rico asked Juicy. She had just stepped out the shower and was on her way to join him in bed. She hadn't been her upbeat, chipper self lately and he knew it had to do with that night in his strip club.

"You don't ever let me in, Rico," she said. "I can't believe you'd tell a nigga you barely know everything about you, but don't tell me shit."

"I ain't tell that nigga everything—"

"Mothafucka, the only thing you *ain't* tell him was your blood type and social security number."

"Watch, your mouth."

"No, *you* watch it. I'm tired of feeling left in the dark. I didn't even know 'til then what your last name was."

"You never asked."

"Don't be a smart ass, Rico. I don't like that shit. I feel like you know everything about me and I know nothing."

Rico pulled her close and held her like a baby. After all, that's what she really wanted. Some attention and a little coddling. "Come here, my queen. What'chu wanna know? Ask and I'll tell."

Rico was accustomed to keeping his innermost thoughts to himself. He'd grown used to only using women for therapeutic release. Never to vent or open up to. He felt like if he showed that vulnerable side of himself the hoes would eat him up and spit him out alive. Because of that, he bottled his emotions and avoided getting too personal with people.

"I wanna know everything," she said.

"I can't tell you everything, baby..."

"Why not?"

"'Cuz I'm tryin' to eat your pussy right now. And that shit would take entirely too long."

"Rico," she whined, playfully hitting his arm. He definitely wasn't taking her as serious as the situation was to her.

"What'chu wanna know, baby?"

"*Something.* Anything."

"Okay, well... Let's see... I was homeless for three years. Sleeping behind a Walmart, going without food. Shit was rough. I had to get up early to wash my ass at the gas station. I finally caught a lil' break when I got a job working at Olive Garden. Anyway, one of my female co-workers started stripping. Said she needed the extra cash. She wanted to know if I could look out for her—be kinda like a body-guard to her—and that's how I got in the game. We started recruiting girls together. We were rollin' in big faces too before she got killed."

"Wow..."

"Yeah, some scumbag robbed and shot her leaving the club."

"That whole story is just...wow, Rico. You been through so much. I didn't know you were homeless."

"That's why I hustle hard the way I do. I never want to experience that level of struggle again. You either gon' boss up or get bossed on."

"I can dig that." Juicy paused for a second. "...Speaking of hustle, do you really think this is the best line of work for Amanda...? I mean... She's just...so... She's really..."

Rico quickly shut her down. "I know all Amanda's screws ain't tight, but she make a lot of fuckin' money. At the end of the day, that's all that matters. It's mothafuckas with college degrees dat ain't doing shit with they lives. I don't give a fuck how fucked up she is. That's *my* mothafuckin' bitch and I ain't ever gon' let her go."

～

ROXIE DASHED around her home like a chicken with its head cut off as she prepared for her and Kwon's fourth date. Since she was running late, she decided to let him wait for her in her apartment.

Roxie hadn't even decided on an outfit yet when she opened her door and invited him inside. She was surprised when she saw him bearing a bouquet of white roses.

"Why thank you," she said before kissing him on the cheek. Every inch of his skin was so smooth and soft.

"Nice place you got here," he said, looking around.

"Thanks. Make yourself comfortable. I'll be ready in a sec. Do you want anything to drink?"

"No, I'm fine. Thanks for offering."

Roxie rushed back to the bedroom and disappeared inside the wardrobe closet to find something to wear. After what felt like an eternity, she finally decided on a black turtleneck dress and cheetah print booties with bloody bottoms. A red Valentino handbag accentuated the outfit perfectly.

Roxie laid the outfit on a chaise as she prepared to touch up herself with makeup.

"I didn't know you had children," Kwon called out from the living room. He noticed the plethora of toys lying on the floor. "Three dates and you haven't told me that once."

There was a slight hint of humor in his voice so she knew he wasn't too offended. She just wanted to get to know him a little better before she got personal.

"Yeah, just one. A little girl. She's with her auntie right now." Cameron wasn't biologically related to Rain but she was the closest thing to an aunt she had. Roxie didn't know any of her baby daddy's relatives—and in her case, that might've been for the best.

"What's her name?" Kwon asked.

"Rain."

"That's a beautiful name. Is this her? On the mantle?" Kwon admired the stormy blue eyes she inherited from her crazy ass uncle.

"Yep. That's my lil' pooder bear," Roxie giggled.

"She looks just like you," he told her.

Roxie laughed. "Everyone always says that."

She slid out of her loungewear and went to her 2-piece vanity set to apply foundation. She didn't notice when Kwon stepped in the doorway. Roxie was wearing nothing but her panties and bra.

When he saw her standing there half-naked, he simply admired her in awe. He'd already saw her assets while she was at work, but it still felt like he was seeing her for the very first time.

Roxie looked up and saw him staring. She immediately became embarrassed because her scars were visible. She didn't like anyone to see her without makeup on.

"Kwon, I—I didn't even here you walk up," she said, nervously. He had the stealth of a ninja, no pun intended.

"Why are you putting that makeup on your body?" he asked, curiously.

Roxie froze up. She didn't want to tell him that her baby daddy's brother had tried to kill her. Maybe one day she would. But it was far too early to now. Plus, she hated revisiting that horrific day.

When she didn't answer right away, Kwon invited himself inside the room.

Roxie tensed up when he closed the space between them. Ever so gently, he trailed his fingers down her arm. She didn't stop him from taking in the full, unadulterated sight of her body. He wasn't at all intimidated by a couple scars. If anything, it only intrigued him. There was a lot more to Roxie than he thought.

Her breath caught in her chest, when he suddenly leaned down and kissed one of them. "You don't have to do that with me," he whispered.

Her sense of confidence grew just hearing him say that.

Kwon gripped her waist and pulled her close to him. When his lips covered hers, she melted in his embrace.

"Kwon," she whispered as he trailed sweet kisses along her neck.

"...Should I stop?" he murmured.

Roxie thought about it for all of two seconds. "No..." Grabbing him by the hand, she led him to her bed, and together they landed on the plush mattress.

Kwon slid in between her legs fully clothed. His delicate touches and kisses were passion-felt and left her in a drunken state of ecstasy. Apart of her felt like they might've been moving too fast, but she didn't care. It was too late to turn back now and she wanted him just as badly as he wanted her.

"I haven't," he suddenly said.

"You haven't what?"

"...I haven't dated a black girl before."

Roxie giggled. "So are you with me right now for the experience?" she asked.

Kwon looked her dead in the eyes with a serious expression. "You know damn well why I'm here, Roxie."

She hesitated. "Kwon, I told you—"

He immediately kissed her into silence. "I don't care about your past. All I want to know is if there's a place for me in your future..."

Kwon kissed every scar on her body before stopping at her waist. "Is there?"

Breathing heavily, Roxie bit her bottom lip and nodded sheepishly. She watched as he pulled her panties off and tossed them to the floor.

Roxie gasped when she felt his warm tongue move smoothly over her clit. "Kwon," she whimpered.

He took his time learning her body, and what she liked. If he noticed her reaction to a certain way he did something, he'd do more of it. Kwon was desperate to please her.

Running her fingers through his silky jet-black hair, she savored the way he kissed and sucked on her button. "Taste good?" she whispered.

Kwon grabbed her thick thighs and buried his face even deeper. "It's the best thing I ever tasted, baby."

After making her squirt off his tongue game, he wiped his wet lips, and climbed in between her legs. Roxie eagerly helped him remove his t-shirt. His entire chest and arms were covered with tattoos. Most of them she didn't understand because they were in Korean. However, if she did know the meanings, she might've ran and never looked back.

Kwon interlocked their fingers and kissed her with the same passion a husband would a wife.

"Kwon, I don't wanna get hurt..."

"I promise, you won't."

"So is it true?" Juicy asked. "You know? What they say about Chinese men?"

"He's not Chinese, bitch. He's Korean," Roxie corrected her.

"Same thing," Juicy shrugged.

"No...it's *really* not."

Cameron laughed at the two women's banter. They were all hanging out at her house, sipping wine, and chatting. Jag had yet to surface since their Walmart run-in, but she knew he was only because he was sitting back plotting.

"So is the saying true or what?" Juicy pressed. "Stop holding out on us."

"Is what true? The stereotype that all Asians have little dicks?" Roxie asked.

"Yes, bitch. I need to know!"

"Juicy, yo' giddy ass acting like *you* wanna fuck!" Cameron teased her.

"I mean, shit, I'm just curious. Aren't you?"

"Do all black guys have big dicks?" Roxie asked Juicy.

"Hell fucking no."

"Okay then, there you have it."

"So...seven inches? ...Eight inches...? ...Nine inches? I'mma keep guessing until you stop me."

Roxie burst out laughing. "Kwon doesn't have a horse dick if that's what you're asking. But it's a great size, and he's very passionate in the bedroom. He likes to kiss a lot."

"Ten inches...? Eleven inches...?" Juicy carried on.

"DIANA!" Cameron shouted.

"Okay, okay." She held her hands up in mock surrender.

"Cameron, I still can't believe you're leaving us," Roxie suddenly said.

"Girl, stop. You know ya'll are more than welcome to come and stay as long as you like."

"I know. It just won't be the same without you."

"You've got Juicy," Cam said. "Her and Pimping Ken should be more than enough entertainment."

Everyone laughed at Juicy's expense and she flipped them off. "Fuck ya'll. I'm getting money and eleven inches every night," she bragged. "So ya'll hoes can kiss my ass."

"Alright now," Cameron said. "Don't say I didn't forewarn you. That nigga is trouble.... I just know it."

Juicy waved Cam off. In her eyes, Rico could do no wrong. "Good thing I handle trouble well," she said, reciting one of his earlier lines. Little did she know, that statement would soon come back to bite her in the ass.

AFTER ANOTHER STEAMY sex session in her apartment, Kwon treated Roxie to Sherry Cobbler cocktails and dessert at *H. Harper Station*. He playfully fed her the fruit from their drinks as they conversed, and occasionally eavesdropped on nearby journalists and politicos. Kwon liked being around her and he loved how down-to-earth she was. He had a hard time believing she was single, and an even harder time figuring out why someone was stupid enough to let her slip away. Roxie was funny, smart, kind, and beautiful. Everything he ever wanted in a woman, and then some. While they laughed and talked about everything under the sun, they were completely oblivious to the angry ex parked outside.

Magyc had his chopper with the extendo clip, and two shooters in the car ready for a battle. He was so drunk and high that he felt like he was sitting next to himself.

Roxie didn't know it, but he had followed her there. Magyc couldn't wait to catch their asses slipping in the parking lot.

"I got somethin' for that slanted eyed, dog-eating mothafucka."

Thirty minutes later, Roxie and Kwon emerged from the restaurant smiling and holding hands like they were already an official couple. Magyc's blood boiled as he watched them interact. It tore him up inside to see that she actually looked happy.

"There go that chopstick chink right there," his homie said in the backseat.

Together, all three men climbed out the car with murderous intentions.

∼

"AYE, wus good? I ain't know we was in the business of makin' new friends."

Roxie and Kwon were a few feet away from his car when Magyc and his niggas approached them. Unfortunately, no witnesses were present in the parking lot, which was exactly how Magyc wanted it.

"Last I checked, you have that leisure once you're single." Roxie wasn't scared of his overly jealous ass. And she damn sure wasn't about to let him punk her new boo.

"That's the fuckin' thing though. You ain't fuckin' single."

"Look, we don't want any trouble," Kwon said. He seemed undaunted by the fact that he was outnumbered.

"I don't think I was talkin' to you, bruh." Magyc looked back at Roxie. "And when you start fuckin' Mr. Miyagi anyway."

"Magyc, you need to fucking gon' 'head with that bullshit," Roxie said. She could clearly see that he was drunk, and looking for someone to blame since she dumped him.

"If you had that mothafucka around my daughter, I swear—"

"She's not your daughter," Roxie interrupted. "She's some dead nigga's baby, remember?"

Magyc's jaw muscle tensed. He didn't have a damn thing to say, and he regretted even letting that stupid shit come out his mouth.

"That lil' girl is mine," he said. "*You're* mine. And I ain't finna let some socket face, eggroll-eating mothafucka come between us."

"That's enough!" Roxie said, taking up for Kwon. "You need to leave! Take your stupid ass friends with you too!"

"Bitch, if I'm leavin' yo' ass comin' with me."

"I'm not going nowhere with you!"

Magyc made a move to grab her, but Kwon quickly stepped in front of her.

"You heard the lady. She doesn't wanna go with you. Why don't you back off?"

Magyc looked at his niggas and then back at Kwon like he was crazy. He had to be for even opening his mouth to him.

"Didn't I just tell yo' mothafuckin' ass this ain't got shit to do wit'chu? This between me and my bitch! You lucky I don't murk yo' ass where you stand." Magyc thought about killing him, but realized he wasn't even worth the ammo. Instead, he'd rather enjoy watching him get beaten to a bloody pulp. "Man, TJ, drop this silly mothafucka. I'm done even talkin'."

TJ handed his gun to Magyc and cracked his neck and knuckles. He'd been a backyard brawler for years prior to working for Jude. He loved a good old fashion fistfight.

Like a bull in a ring, TJ charged full speed at Kwon, preparing to tackle him—

Wwwhhmppp!

Kwon sent his ass flying backwards with an unexpected side kick that might've left TJ bleeding internally.

His body slammed hard into a nearby car, shattering the passenger window. He was snoring before he even hit the ground. No one present anticipated that—not even Roxie. With all the conversing they did inside the restaurant, Kwon failed to mention he was a 4th degree black belt.

Magyc and his homie, Sean looked at each other in bewilderment.

"Magyc, just get your fucking friend and go," Roxie insisted.

"Nah, fuck that. Sean, handle that nigga."

Sean looked somewhat nervous but still posted up with Kwon. He threw an uncoordinated punch that Kwon easily ducked.

"Magyc, stop!" Roxie hollered.

Sean threw another punch and missed.

"I don't wanna hurt you," Kwon said, calmly.

"That's too bad," Sean said. "'Cuz I'm finna crush yo' ass and make sushi outta you."

"Magyc, make him stop!" Roxie cried.

He ignored her please as he patiently waited for Kwon to be dealt with.

Sean threw yet another punch and missed.

"I said I don't wanna hurt," Kwon repeated.

It was three of them and not a single one could get a hit in.

Fed up that Kwon was making him look like a bitch, Sean tried to catch him off guard with a kick of his own.

Kwon blocked the attack with his leg before brutally kicking Sean's knee out of place.

Sean dropped to the ground like a sack of bricks, howling in pain.

"AHH, SHIT! FUCK! This mothafucka broke my gotdamn leg! FUCK!"

Magyc glared at Kwon, and the two simply stared daggers at each other.

Magyc wanted to run up, but he'd already seen what Kwon did to his niggas. He wasn't going to waste time or energy sparring—especially when he knew he'd probably get his ass kicked. Magyc didn't know a thing about Martial Arts other than the Kung Fu movies he saw growing up. He had a feeling that if he tried to fight Kwon he would only embarrass himself in the process. So instead of squaring up like a man, he pointed his pistol at Kwon—

"No!" Roxie quickly leapt in front of Kwon, almost taking the bullet for him. "STOP! Enough is enough! Just let it go! It's over!"

"It ain't fuckin' over—"

"It's over!"

Hearing her say that hurt Magyc more than anything. As bad as he wanted to pull the trigger, he knew that wouldn't win her back. This would be a life lesson for him. Magyc fucked up, and now he had to watch another man make her happy.

"WHY DIDN'T you tell me you knew Karate?" Roxie asked him on the way back to her apartment.

Kwon didn't take his eyes off the road as he navigated his car. "Because I don't know karate," he said. "That back there was a combination of Taekwondo and Wing Chun."

"Where did you learn that?"

"My grandfather taught me at a very early age. In my family, it is mandatory to be skilled in mixed martial arts or some type of combat."

"Why?"

"Because...I...it's just the way it is," he said.

"Why do I get the impression you're hiding something from me, Kwon?"

Silence was the response she received.

"You're not a DJ, are you?" she finally said.

"No, Roxie...I'm not..."

The rest of the trip was quiet. Roxie didn't speak again until they finally arrived in front of her building.

"Are you gonna tell me what you really do? Or will I be left wondering—just like I'm wondering why you lied in the first place."

Kwon could tell she was upset but that wasn't his intentions. "I didn't want to tell you the truth, because I didn't want you to think differently of me," he admitted.

"Well, I do regardless, because now I know you're a liar..."

He went to touch her hand and she quickly moved it away.

"I am sorry that I lied to you, Roxie."

She heard the sincerity in his tone, but she wouldn't fold.

"The truth is... I have my hands in some pretty heavy shit."

"Like the Yakuza?" she laughed, half-joking half-serious.

There was no humor in his tone when he said, "...Something like that..." Kwon couldn't come out and say he was a member and the heir to a notorious Asian criminal enterprise.

After seeing the seriousness on his face, she wiped the smile off of hers. Roxie wasn't particularly happy about dating another criminal.

She'd lost three men to that street shit, and she didn't want to lose another.

"Roxie, I'm sorry..."

"I am too," she said. "I don't think I can do this again." She reached for the door handle but he stopped her.

"What are you saying?"

"I'm saying that I can't do this with you. You lied to me, Kwon, and if it's one thing I hate it's a liar. I just got out of a relationship that was plagued by lies. I don't wanna step into another—"

"You won't," he assured her.

"I know I won't because it's not gonna happen."

Kwon looked crushed.

Roxie went to climb out again but he gently grabbed her wrist.

"It's not often I find this," he said, in reference to their chemistry. "Don't throw it away. I know if you give me the chance, I could really make you happy. And I promise I will keep my business life far away from you and your daughter."

"I'm sorry, but that just isn't enough," she said. Suddenly, it dawned on her that maybe she was meant to be single. She could use the moment of solitude to find herself and focus on her child. Roxie was done playing the role of a trap queen. She had a baby to raise. "Goodbye, Kwon."

He barely wanted to let her go when she climbed out his car. Roxie was the closest thing to perfection he'd met in a woman and now she was walking away. Unfortunately, Kwon had no choice but to accept and respect it.

23

J uicy, Milena, Flo, and Kina walked in the house from a long
day of shopping and hanging out. Every day they were in the
city running a stupid check up. They had fun and did everything together like a group of girls in high school.

Juicy let herself in since Rico gave her the key to their home. He
was currently in Europe for business, so she was holding shit down in
Atlanta. Just as she stepped in, Rico Face Timed her.

"Wassup, bay?"

"Me and the girls just walked in."

"Word? Lemme see what'chu wearin' today? I miss yo' fine ass."

Juicy lowered the camera so he could see her tan jumpsuit and
knee-high Givenchy boots.

"Damn, my bitch bad," he said. "How my ladies doing
over there?"

Juicy moved the camera so the girls could wave.

"I'mma see you in a couple days. I got you a gift too."

"What'd you get me?"

"If I told you it wouldn't be a gift, now would it."

Juicy laughed.

"I'm finna get up outta here though. Gimme a kiss."

Juicy puckered her lips and blew him a kiss. She was about to disconnect the call, but he quickly said something that caught her off guard.

"Aye...I love you, girl."

"...I love you too."

"Get at'chu later," he said before hanging up.

As Juicy walked further in the house, she heard the faint sound of a baby crying.

"What the hell is that?"

"Amanda must be watching those God awful shows again."

"She got the TV on max though?" Juicy asked.

Milena shrugged and walked off to her bedroom. No more than two seconds later, the noises stopped.

Juicy dismissed it and went to the kitchen to fix herself something to eat. When she walked inside, she slipped and almost bust her ass on something wet. As soon as she looked down, her body froze up.

There was a trail of blood leading to—

"AMANDA, NOOOOOO! What did you do?!" Juicy was horrified and mentally scarred by what she saw. The gruesome scene before her would haunt her at night for many years to come.

"I—I just wanted to go to the doctor's appointment with her," she said in a dreamy voice. "She wouldn't let me... I just wanted to go with her. All I wanted was to see the baby... That's all I ever wanted was a baby of my own...and now I finally have one..."

Amanda sadistically held up the bloody newborn baby in her hands. The tiny premature infant had just stopped breathing after she stabbed Delaney to death and cut it out of her.

Juicy looked at Delaney's body stretched out on the floor and covered her mouth to keep from being sick. Her body was completely mutilated. Blood, bodily fluids, puss, and intestines covered the floor.

Juicy almost couldn't believe what she was seeing. *This is not real. This is not fucking real*, she told herself repeatedly. But every time she blinked, the shocking image remained.

Just then Milena walked in the kitchen to see what all the ruckus was about. "What the hell is—OH MY GOD! Oh—Oh my God! OH NO! No, no, no, no! DELANEY!"

Flo and Kina ran in the kitchen next. The minute Flo saw the mess she threw up all over the kitchen tile.

Milena quickly ran out of the room to call 911.

"NOOOOOOOOO!"

"Delaney!"

"Why? Amanda, why?!"

Kina ran over to check Delaney's pulse, but it was no use. Judging from the stiffness of her body and dull pigmentation, she had been dead for quite some time.

Before Juicy could get a wrap on the situation, she heard sirens wailing in the distance.

"Shit!"

Juicy pulled out her phone and immediately called Rico.

He answered on the fourth ring. "Wassup, bay?"

"I don't know what to do, Rico! I don't know what the fuck to do! Tell me what to do!" she cried frantically.

"Calm down and talk to me. What happened?"

"It's Amanda! I—she—"

"What happened?!" Rico asked.

"She—she killed Delaney!"

"WHAT!"

Just then Juicy heard the police and FBI storm the premises.

"Oh my God, Rico! What do I do? The cops are here!"

"Hol' up! The Feds there right now?!" he asked in disbelief.

"Yes!" She heard their heavy footsteps coming straight towards them. "What do I do, Rico! I—I'm so scared! I—"

Click.

Rico hung up on her silly ass, leaving her and the girls to fend for themselves. Juicy's worst fears had come to life. Cameron tried to warn her about Rico but she just wouldn't listen. She'd never considered the consequences because she was too busy fucking, making money, and having fun.

Juicy wanted to run from herself and she ran right into the arms of a manipulative womanizer. She had no idea what she had stepped into by agreeing to work with Rico. And she had no clue as to why the officers slapped the cuffs on her *and* Amanda.

"I didn't do anything!" Juicy screamed. "I didn't do any fucking thing! Why are you arresting me?! SHE'S THE KILLER! Not me! I didn't do shit!" Once she became hostile, the police slammed her roughly to the floor.

Delaney's blood smeared all over her face and clothes. This would go down in history as the worst day in her life—and she had no one but herself to blame.

~

"CAN I COME IN?"

Tara stepped to the side to allow Magyc entrance. He had an over-sized bag from Toys R Us with him.

"What's the occasion?" she asked grimly. "I didn't expect to see you again after our fall out."

"I just came by to give lil' man this," he said, handing her the bag. He would've given it to Marlon himself but he was in daycare. "I also came to apologize about everything. I ain't trying to fight with you, Tara. And I ain't trying to no deadbeat like my father was. I wanna do more—no I'm *gonna* do more," he stressed.

Tara smiled.

"I am still firm on wanting to be just friends," he added. "We have to be cordial for the baby."

"I agree. And I can live with that."

Magyc was actually surprised to hear her say that. Usually, Tara would flip if he said some shit he didn't like. But after taking some time to think and contemplate her past actions, she realized how childish she'd been.

"I'm sorry too," Tara said. "I should've never did what I did. I wish I could take it back."

"Well, it's over and done with now. Ain't shit to do put keep it pushing so we can take care of our kids."

"Kid," she corrected him. "I got the abortion..."

Magyc was floored by the news. As soon as he saw the tears in fill up in her eyes he walked over and held her. Just because he wasn't in love with Tara didn't mean he had to disrespect her. He planned on being a better person, and a better father.

IT WAS FINALLY the big day. Cameron and Jude were getting ready to move to their Hawaii retreat. They had already packed and shipped everything, and she was waiting on him to return with the moving truck. For all the things she didn't plan on taking she wanted to give away.

Cameron kept herself busy cleaning the house. She didn't want to leave it untidy before moving since they planned on selling it. They already had a few potential buyers interested in taking a look, and she wanted the place to be in tip top shape.

Cam was listening to music on her Amazon Echo and sweeping the lower level when she heard the doorbell ring. Jude had left her with one of his men, so she assumed he'd locked himself out. It wouldn't have been the first time.

Turning down the volume, Cam sauntered to the front door. Before she could look through the peephole, it flew open, and slammed into her face. Caught off guard, Cam fell backward, clutching her bloody nose. She wouldn't have been surprised if her shit was broken.

When Cam looked up and saw Jag hovering over her with clenched fists, she knew the end was near.

Cameron quickly scurried to her purse where her loaded gun was—but Jag grabbed her by the leg and pulled her back towards him. The door was wide open and she could see Jude's dead homeboy lying several feet away with a bullet in his head. Something as simple as taking the trash out for Cam had cost him his life.

"Jag, no! STOP!"

"You thought it was over?" he asked. "You really thought it was fucking over?"

She kicked him in the shin when he got to close. Apparently, that pissed him off because he grabbed a wire hanger off the floor and started beating her.

"Who's gonna love you more than me?!"

WHAP

"Huh?"

WHAP!

Who?" he hollered.

The wired hanger left welts on her bare skin.

"That mothafucka will never love or care about you the way I do! Did you really think I was gonna let him take you from me?! Bitch, you belong to me!"

"LEAVE ME ALONE!"

Jag tossed the hanger and snatched his leather belt off. Since he wasn't on meds he was twice as deranged as she remembered.

"Yo' mothafuckin' ass ain't goin' nowhere, bitch! I can't believe you even had the gall to think you'd leave me!"

WHAM!

Jag punched her in the face and body with the belt wrapped around his fist. When he didn't feel satisfied doing that, he wrapped it around her neck and choked her. He didn't intend to kill her. He just wanted to let her know who was in control. He would tame her, one way or another.

"I'll die before I let him take you from me!"

With the belt wrapped around her neck, he dragged her out the house and towards his car. Since she was wearing a skirt, her arms and legs painfully scraped against the ground. She was kicking and screaming the entire way. She couldn't breathe, and she feared she'd die before she even made it to the car.

Every so often she tried to stand, but fell back down unmercifully. Suddenly, Cameron remembered that her babies were inside alone.

"NO, JAG, PLEASE! she struggled to say. "My children—"

"Bitch, fuck yo' children!" he spat. "That's exactly what them mothafuckas is—*yo'* children! Let that fucker raise 'em and be grateful I showed mercy 'cuz I could've buried all ya'll mothafuckin' asses!"

All of a sudden, God answered her prayers, when she saw Jude's rental truck pull in. As soon as he saw Jag assaulting Cam he jumped out, forgetting to put it in park. The truck continued rolling before crashing into his precious Ferrari. He didn't give a fuck about that car or anything. All he cared about was protecting his wife.

"GET THE FUCK AWAY FROM MY GIRL!"

Jude couldn't believe Jag was actually alive. He wanted to kick himself for not believing Cameron when she tried to tell him.

Both men pulled their guns out at the same time, and Cam immediately thought the worse.

"I was supposed to kill you a long time ago," Jag said. "Bitch, the only reason you still breathin' is 'cuz of Cameron. I gave yo' ass the benefit of the doubt, but you weren't even worth that."

"Fuck you! I'mma put'cho ass in the ground right next to yo' brother."

Jag didn't like that at all. Feeling insanely bold, he tossed his gun to the ground, ready to fight like a man. Jude had ample opportunity to put lead in his brain—but instead he tossed his too.

As soon as both men were weaponless, Jag charged at him full speed. He tackled Jude like a linebacker, delivering fierce blow after blow.

Cameron ran up to try and help her man, and Jag shoved the shit out of her. She fell and smacked her head so hard that she saw double.

WHAM!

WHAM!

WHAM!

"I shoulda gutted yo' mothafuckin' ass and left you in the woods somewhere to die!" Jag yelled. "All of the shit you did to me!"

WHAM!

"You don't deserve her!"

WHAM!

"You never fuckin' did! That's gon' always be my bitch! She always gon' suck this dick! And I'mma always fuck her and eat her pussy! And it ain't shit you can do about it, mothafucka!" Jag wanted to psychologically torture Jude as he assaulted him. He didn't care that his words were bizarre and outrageous.

THUNK!

Cameron suddenly hit him over the head with a nearby shovel.

Thankfully, it was enough to get him off Jude—but not enough to kill him.

Jag stood and snatched the shovel out her hand. She thought he might hit her with it, but instead he slapped the blood out her mouth.

That automatically pissed Jude off. Seeing his girl get hit, made him jump off the ground and slam Jag from behind. Now it was his turn to go in. He pummeled Jag's face until his knuckles turned red and bled.

Cameron crawled over to where Jag's gun fell and grabbed it. When she looked at the chamber it was empty. He only had the one bullet he used on Jude's homie. He never intended to shoot. He just wanted to disarm his enemy.

After he exhausted himself from punching, Jude wearily stood to his feet and proceeded to stomp Jag. He kicked him all in the chest, face, and torso. By the time he finished giving it to him good Jag was barely recognizable.

Jude tired himself out so much that he collapsed beside him winded.

The crazy mothafucka actually had the nerve to laugh.

"You think this shit's a game?" he asked. Jude climbed on top of Jag and proceeded to strangle him.

Cam lightly touched his shoulder to make him stop. At first, Jude thought she might actually want to spare this fucker like she did with Alessia. He was surprised to see his gun in her hand. She wanted him to finish it once and for all.

Jude stood to his feet and pointed the gun at Jag. One of his eyes were swollen shut, his nose was twisted at an awkward angle, and his lips were swollen and cut.

Jag still seemed unfazed. There was a devilish grin on his face. "You think a bullet will make it stop?" he asked Jude. "Mothafucka, even if I'm dead I'll still be in her dreams. When you fuckin' her I'mma be on her mind. It never goes away," he said. "*I never go away.*"

Jude cocked the gun. He was tired of listening to Jag talk about himself like he was a God. He was about to find out just how mortal he really was.

"Your kids will remember me as their first father." Jag laughed maniacally. "Don't you get it?" he asked. "I win...even if I lose."

When Cam noticed that his words were getting to Jude she snatched the gun out his hand herself. She'd heard enough.

Jag looked at her and started laughing. "I'll see you in hell, bitch—"

POP!

POP!

POP!

POP!

POP!

POP!

Cameron emptied the entire clip into his face, silencing Jag forever.

EPILOGUE

Sadly, Juicy realized the truth and error of her ways when it was far too late. Sitting in court, she felt like a damn fool as each girl testified to her running a human trafficking ring.

Every single one got on the stand and lied; Milena, Flo, and Kina. Hell, even Amanda—who was charged with 1st degree murder—hopped on the snitch bandwagon.

If it wasn't for the baby being rushed to the hospital in time, she would've been facing a double homicide instead.

None of the girls would dare snitch on their beloved Rico—and instead Juicy was the one who had to take the fall. All along, he'd been conditioning her to go down should the day ever come.

The truth was, Rico never knew T, had never visited Cleveland, and had lied about damn near everything—except being homeless. He'd done his homework on her, well before he even opened his mouth to say hi. Rico was fully aware that she was a mega stripper in her hometown, and he knew of her hustle via social media.

He didn't have to do much research. At least not enough to seem stalkerish. The streets talked. And he knew having a bitch like her on his team would only pay off in the end.

It certainly did.

Rico put the house rental and club in her name without her knowing. That was the only real reason he gave a fuck about her government. It wasn't hard at all to pin the trafficking charges on her.

It also turned out that Amanda was only 16. Juicy couldn't believe that Rico had lied to her about her age. Because she wasn't an adult, Juicy was additionally charged with exploiting a minor for sexual purposes, possession of depictions of minors, promoting sex with minors, and conspiracy to promote travel for the purpose of sex with minors.

The judge threw the book at Juicy after calling her every filthy, slanderous term he could think of. Thirty years was what she received—despite yelling his name out in the court room repeatedly, further embarrassing herself.

On top of that, she was charged in connection to Wayne's untimely murder. Juicy didn't even know he was dead. Apparently, Rico's girls had done some slick shit to help pin it on her, should the Feds come sniffing.

Juicy was so naïve and clueless. All the while, she was kicking it with them thinking they were friends, they were ready and willing to throw her under the bus at a moment's notice.

Juicy would be pushing 60 by the time she saw the light of day again, and Rico's girls got nothing but fines, community service, and a slap on the wrist. And that mothafucka was probably somewhere with his feet kicked up laughing at her dumb ass.

What was most sad, above everything else, was Juicy finding out she was 3 weeks pregnant after being booked. Not only would she rot in the system, she wouldn't even be able to raise her own child. It'd be ripped away from her the day it was born just like Delaney.

All that time Juicy thought Rico was a rider. But he had fucked her raw with no Vaseline. She'd gotten the shitty end of the stick, and she had to walk that sad journey alone.

Love was a mothafucka.

~

ROXIE WAS PLAYING with Rain when someone knocked on her door. Jude and Cameron had already moved so she wasn't sure who the visitor was. At first, she thought it was Magyc still trying to come around and make amends. For the most part, he did his best to respect her space, but he still had a hard time letting go.

Roxie was pleasantly surprised to see Kwon instead. She should've known he wasn't going to give up that easily. Roxie wondered how life would go if she didn't open the door and if they continued their lives without each other. After all, she wasn't ready to let another man in. But she'd be lying if she said she wasn't just a little bit curious about him.

What the hell, a tiny voice in her head said. *You only live once.*

Kwon looked like he had hit the lottery when she opened the door and smiled at him.

CAMERON AND JUDE were relaxing together on the patio of their beautiful Hawaii home without a care in the world. The children were safe, their lives were drama free and best of all, there was no more Jag. No more feeling like she had to look over her shoulder, or be on her guards 24/7. After years of painful relationships, heartache, and abuse, it felt good to finally be happy.

As promised, Jude passed the torch down to Magyc. He left him two sound pieces of advice. *A boss creates fear, and a leader creates confidence. And buy or bury the competition.* Magyc may've been a little hot-headed and uneven at times, but so was Jude when he first started out. He had a lot of faith in his protégée.

Cameron reached over and slid her hand in Jude's. He looked over at her and winked and it made her whole world seem perfect. Cam had helped him become a better man. His whole life changed the day she smiled at him. Cameron was 100% down for him. She'd been with him at his highest point and even at his lowest. She had his back when he wasn't on top, and helped him get to where he was. If it was in God's will they'd be together forever.

CAMERON 8: THE FINALE IS OUT NOW! VISIT —>
http://amzn.to/2zHGsqW

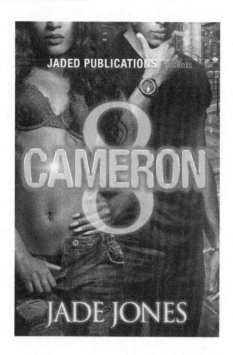

CONTINUE READING ABOUT THE GANG IN "WIFE OF A MISFIT"

AVAILABLE NOW!